The Kryptonite Kid

a novel by

Joseph Torchia

THE KRYPTONITE KID

Holt, Rinehart and Winston   New York

An Owl Book

C. 2

for Sandy & Sog

Library of Congress Cataloging in Publication Data
Torchia, Joseph.
The Kryptonite kid.
I. Title.
PZ4.T684Kr [PS3570.067]   813'.5'4   79–1078
ISBN Hardbound: 0–03–046676–8
ISBN Paperback: 0–03–057798–5

First published in hardcover by Holt, Rinehart and Winston in 1979.
First Owl Book Edition—1980.

DESIGNER: *Joy Chu*
Printed in the United States of America
1 3 5 7 9 10 8 6 4 2

NOV 4 '80

"We are the children of our landscape . . ."
　　　—Lawrence Durrell: Justine

The Kryptonite Kid

I've been having tons of crisp dreams lately, waking with the sunlight and remembering every horrid detail. They're full of heavy chunks of past, of old faces floating through the air, exploding into punctuation marks. Every night they occur, like mosquitoes biting into my sleep, leaving marks that will itch all morning, all afternoon, all the way into evening, by which time I feel a compulsion to record them. But when I sit down at my desk and confront an empty sheet of paper, they run away like children. I chase them and they laugh. I sip my coffee. I nervously light a cigarette. I say a prayer. I bless myself. I slide between my sheets and crawl inside my sleep with certainty. I know they will come again. I know they will find me . . .

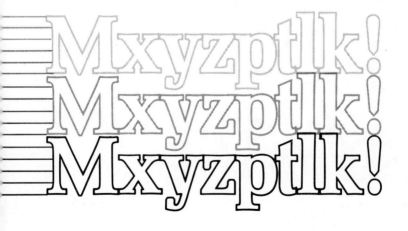

The
First
Dimension

Dear Superman,

It's me again. Remember I wrote you a letter a long time ago and you never wrote back? Robert said maybe it got lost or else maybe you already wrote it and we didn't get it yet. Or else maybe you forgot about it except you never forget because you got a Super brane. That's why I'm writing again. Because we always buy all your comic-books even the special big GIANT issues that cost a lot more. And we never miss your television program on TV and that's why we think you should write us a letter this time. And then if we ever find any Kryptonite around we'll throw it in the Clarion River so it don't kill you on our way to school. Goodby.

Your friends,
Jerry Chariot and Robert Sipanno

———

Dear Clark Kent,

I hope you don't mind if I call you Clark Kent but I'll make sure to put your REAL name on the outside of the envelope so nobody will know who you really aren't. And besides I don't think anybody will read this letter unless he's a criminel. Anyway, the main reason I'm writing again is to ask if you used to wear diapers when you was Superbaby in Smallville which was way before Ma and Pa Kent got poisoned to death and you thought it was your fault but it really wasn't. Me and Robert just finished the story called THE TRAGIC DAY MA AND PA KENT DIED in GIANT SUPERBOY NO. 165 and I cried like you did. And so did Robert. Especially on page 10 where you took your foster mother's dead hand and said to her dead body, "Mother!—Her pulse . . . It's stopped! She's gone! Gone! Choke!" And then your foster father said, "You must always use your Super powers to do good . . . uphold law and order! Good luck, my son . . . And goodbye!" And then he died also. And you was standing in the cemetery on the top of page 11. I hope you remember. Anyway, if you wore diapers, did you wear them to fool the neighbors when they came by to give your mother presents for you? Or did you really have to wear diapers because you was a real baby even though you was a Superbaby? We hope you'll tell us this time.

Your pals,
Jerry and Robert

PS: Doesn't it bother you when they write stories about what you did when you was littler and just SUPERBOY and not SUPERMAN? I know it would bother me if they wrote about me when I was little. Especially if it was something I didn't want anybody to know. Especially my mom.

———⊷⊶———

Dear SUPERMAN,

Last night at supper I decided to tell my mom how Superman might be writing me a letter pretty soon from Metropolis. And she said WHO? And I said Superman. And my mom said SUPERMAN? And my big brother Buster started to laugh. And my mom said there isn't no Superman because he's just makebelieve like Goldilocks and Little Red Riding Hood. And I said that's really DUMB because you wear a cape instead of a hood. And besides, Little Red Riding Hood is just a story and you're a real person except you're a SUPER person which is even better. That's what I said. You should've heard me. Right in front of my dad and everybody. Only my dad wasn't listening because he was reading the newspaper because that's what he always does when he's eating. My brother Buster laughed again and spit a piece of pork chop at me and called me a DUMMIE. And so my mom hit him. And so Buster kicked me under the table when my mom wasn't looking. I don't think you would like Buster very much even though I know you like everybody a hole lot. Anyway, my mom said Superman is also a story. And I said No sir. And she said Why would I lie to you? And I said I haven't figured that out yet. And Buster said DUMMIE again. And my dad said Pass the potatoes please. And my mom said how that kid has quite a imagination. And I was really getting mad, Superman. And so I said YES SIR THERE IS TOO A SUPERMAN BECAUSE I CAN SEE HIM ON TELEVISION AND BESIDES I KNOW EVERYTHING ABOUT HIM! I was yelling real loud and that's why I wrote it in big letters. I didn't like to cry in front of Buster but I couldn't help it because everybody was looking at me even my dad. He wasn't even reading the newspaper. He was looking right in my eyes. Then he pushed the chair back and stood up and I thought he was gonna come over and hit me with the newspaper. Usually he hits me with his hand but this time he picked up the newspaper and so that's what I thought he was gonna do. Instead he opened it up and put it right in front of me and said, "Who's that?"

It was a picture of you, Superman.

"C'mon," my father said, tapping me on the shoulder with his thick, hard fingers. "C'mon, who is it?"

His voice was deep and scary, but not loud. It was his special voice, the one he used on the day we got report cards in school. Even Buster was quiet.

I was trapped.

I knew he wanted me to say it's Superman and that's why I didn't want to say it's Superman, Superman. But it WAS you. You was standing out in front of the Daily Planet with Lois Lane. It was just after she got pushed out the window and you had to fly down and save her again. I saw that program three times. They even had the same picture in TV Guide once and I cut it out and saved it. That's what I told him. And you know what he told me, Superman? He told me you were dead.

"See that?" he said, pointing a finger at the newspaper. "You can read. It says Superman is dead. It says he shot himself in the head."

I tried to read it but I couldn't because my eyes were all watery and my nose was running and I knew he was gonna hit me. I knew it. But I didn't care because I just didn't because I was mad. I was so mad I couldn't even talk. And so I had to yell. And I DID yell! I told him how he was a LIER and how that was the STUPIDEST thing I ever heard in my life! I told him how nothing can kill Superman except Kryptonite, like the time somebody tried to stab you with a Kryptonite sword. Then I laughed. I laughed real loud. Except I didn't really laugh because my dad doesn't usually lie. And that's when he hit me. That's when he told me how that guy on TV is just a actor and not Superman because there isn't a Superman at all. And there never was and there never will be. And maybe there won't even be a Superman on TV anymore because he committed suicide.

Suicide is when somebody murders yourself. That's what he said when I asked him. Then he said I had to get right upstairs to bed young man and if I ever yelled at the supper table again then he was gonna give me something to yell about. Then he gave me something to yell about anyway. Right across the face. Only I didn't yell, Superman. I didn't even cry. I just went upstairs and I thought about it for a long time and then I thought about it some more and then I decided to write this letter and ask you something. Except I can't right now. Because I'm supposed to be asleep and I just heard my dad turn off the television and so that means I better get in bed right away. Goodnight.

Good mourning, Superman. How are you today? We are fine thank you. I told Robert all about what happend last night and we talked about it for a LONG time and we decided something. We decided that it MUST be a actor on TV and not really you since you're too busy chasing down Mr. Mxyzptlk! and blowing out forest fires to take the time to be on TV or to write us a letter. I knew all along that it wasn't really you because why would you kill yourself when you won't even let anybody else do it? And everybody knows you've had LOTS of chances to do that. But I don't understand why that guy on TV murdered himself because if I ever got the chance to be you I sure wouldn't murder my self no siree. Which is what I wanted to ask you about, Superman. You see, I was thinking that pretty soon they're gonna need somebody else to be Superman on TV and maybe you could ask them to pick me. If you want. And I also thought it might be a good idea if you flew over my house someday when you happen to be out flying around anyway. And if you did it about 5 o'clock in the afternoon then you could wave at my dad when he was coming home from work. Thanks, Man of Steel.

Your Very Good Friends,
JERRY and ROBERT

———✦———

Dear Superfriend,

I know I'm a little little right now but I grow pretty fast. And besides, I already know everything about you like all the different kinds of Kryptonite and The Phantom Zone and stuff like that. And me and Robert always say things like GREAT CAESAR'S GHOST! and HOLY KRYPTON! when we're in our Secret Hiding Place which is a LOT like your Fortress of Solitude. Only it isn't in the Arctic like yours because it's back near Old Lady Holbrook's spring. And last year I got to play The Baby Jesus in the Christmas play and so I can already act. And Robert said to tell you that he was one of the Three Wise Men and so if Jimmy Olsen ever shoots himself then maybe Robert could become Jimmy because he already has freckles anyway. Of course I didn't have any words to say in the play because I was just a Baby. But when Janie Jobb who was my mother The Virgin Mary bent down over my manger I got to cry. And then the shepherds came and I had to be quiet while they prayed to me. Everybody said I was REAL good, even my mom and Sister Mary Justin who picked me. The reason she picked me was because I'm smaller than anybody else in the class except Donna Gapinski who's a girl. Girls don't count because Jesus was a boy. And since I would rather get to be you than The Baby Jesus anyway I thought maybe you could keep me in mind. And also Robert. And then we wouldn't even care if you didn't get a chance to fly over my

house at 5 o'clock which I hope you didn't forget about.
Thank you. Robert says thank you also. Goodby.

JERRY and ROBERT again

PS: Robert said he would like to write you letters like me
only he can't spell as good and so he don't. He said he
hopes it's OK if we write to you together and he hopes
that's not the reason you never answer back.

———✂———

Dear SUPERman,

The other day I took off my shirt and put it around my
neck like a cape and I jumped out of Old Lady Holbrook's
apple tree and I flew. You can even ask Robert. I didn't go
very far but even Robert said it was farther than when I'm
just jumping. I thought you should know that in case
you're still thinking about if you want me to be Superman
on TV. So long.

Your friend JERRY

PS: Robert said to tell you he noticed a couple more
freckles when he got up this morning on his face.

———✂———

Dear Man of Tomorrow,

Yesterday I was taking a bath in the bathtub and I was
reading GIANT SUPERMAN NO. 222 which was about
how you fell in love with Sally Selwyn when Buster came
in to squeez some pimples allover the mirror. I thought it
was really neat how Sally didn't know you was really

13

Superman and so she loved you for yourself and not for everything else. I love you for yourself also. So does Robert. But Buster don't. That's why he sneaked over and grabbed my comicbook and I said YOU BETTER GIVE IT BACK! And he said WHO'S GONNA MAKE ME? And I said ME. And he said GO AHEAD AND TRY. And I said I'LL SPLASH YOU! and he said YOU BETTER NOT! and I said THEN GIVE IT BACK! And he said NO and so I splashed him. And he got real mad. He pushed me under the water and he said SEE, YOU COULD DROWND, EVERYBODY COULD DROWND EVEN SUPERMAN BECAUSE THERE AIN'T NO SUPERMAN, DUMMIE! And I got water up my nose and I tried to hit him but he's too big and I really hated the way he laughed and said DUMMMMMMMMIE just like a girl. Boy that made me mad. So I was wondering if you could get that machine from your Fortress of Solitude and project him into The Phantom Zone where he'll become invisible and disappear. And then when he learns how bad he is you could let him come back to Earth. I hope you like that idea. Thank you again.

Your Pal,
JERRY

Dear SUPERMAN,

I guess things don't look too good, huh? I mean about Superman and television and how I might be in it. Well, I'm glad to know you're trying if you are.

JERRY CHARIOT

PS: Are you?

14

Dear Superman,

Pretty soon we're gonna be making our First Holy Communion and so we have to go to church a lot because we're gonna be making our First Holy Confession also. So we have to learn about sins and how to confess them and so that's why we go to the church. And the other day while we was in church we was supposed to pretend that we was getting ready to tell our sins and we was supposed to be thinking about them and praying. Well, since I couldn't think of very many I decided to read the latest SUPERMAN'S PAL JIMMY OLSEN NO. 163 which happend to be in my notebook. That's the one where you're flying through Jimmy Olsen's window but you couldn't find him because he was all shrunk up and trapped inside that bottle. If you don't remember then maybe you could ask Jimmy about it because if that ever happend to me I sure wouldn't forget about it. And when I was on page 4 where Jimmy gets thrown back through the Time Barrier that's where somebody whisperd JEROME! real loud.

Well, there's only one person who whispers like that and it's Sister Mary Justin. And besides, she's the only one who's allowed to talk at all in church. And besides, she's the only one who calls me Jerome. All my friends call me Jerry. And so does my mom. I consider you a friend even if you hardly ever write back, Superman. But that's OK.

Anyway, when I heard that I knew I was in for it. So did Robert who always sits beside me because he's the second shortest boy in the class. And I knew it was REALLY bad when Sister Mary Justin never said a word all the way back to Holy Redeemer School. Which is right nextdoor to Holy Redeemer Church. Which is across the street from Holy Redeemer Convent. And when we got back in the classroom, we said our morning prayers again to thank God we got back allright from the church where we thanked him we got back allright from the school. And after we finished praying, she put her hands under the white bib of her uniform where she hides her pens and roserys and things. And every time she puts her hands there, that means something really bad is gonna happen. And then it happend.

SUPERMAN! she said, and she said it so loud that everybody jumped even Albert Ambrozzi who has to wear a transister radio thing in his ear and who always talks real loud and so everybody's gonna know all his sins when he crawls in the booth and makes his First Holy Confession.

SUPERMAN IN CHURCH! IN CHURCH! IN CHURCH!

The last time she said CHURCH! like I had committed a Mortal Sin which is the worst kind there is. It's kinda like Green Kryptonite and it means you're going to Hell. With venial sins you just go to Purgatory which is sort of like The Phantom Zone where everybody is invisible. I don't know too much about Heaven yet and I think she's saving that for the end.

I SIMPLY CAN'T BELIEVE IT! she said, and everybody knew she did believe it especially me. The reason I'm putting all her words in BIG letters is because she always talks loud. Except in church where she whispers loud.

THIS IS THE FIRST THING YOU'VE GOT TO CONFESS! she said. YOU BETTER PRAY YOU DON'T GET HIT BY A CAR WHEN YOU LEAVE SCHOOL BECAUSE IF YOU DIE YOU'LL GO STRAIGHT TO HELL!

And let me tell you, Superman, Hell is a lot like Krypton on the day it blew up in GIANT SUPERMAN NO. 222 page 10. It's all hot and red and burning. And you sweat a lot and your skin starts on fire and you want to die but you can't because you're already dead. So you have to live there forever and ever and maybe even longer.

YOU BETTER PRAY YOU LIVE TO MAKE YOUR FIRST HOLY CONFESSION! YOU BETTER PRAY EVERY MINUTE YOU HAVE!

She was standing right next to me and I looked over at Robert and watched him cry as he looked and watched me cry. Me and Robert do everything together. He's my bestfriend. That's when she said I was a SINNER and I had committed a SACRILEDGE and I'd be really lucky if God decided to forgive me.

SUPERMAN IN THE HOUSE OF GOD! she said again and I was really mad. Boy was I mad! But I couldn't do nothing because I was crying too hard.

And just then she grabbed the comicbook and teared it up and threw it in the air and a piece of Jimmy Olsen's head floated down on my desk and I felt a really hard BANG! on the back of my head and I got real dizzie. It was like when I got stung by a bee when me and Robert was in our Secret Hiding Place back near Old Lady Holbrook's spring and it really hurt. I had seen her hit other kids like that but she never hit me like that before and I hope she never does it again. But I think she will because once she doesn't like you then she NEVER likes you because that's the way nunns are. She said she was gonna tell the Principle and she said she was gonna call my mom and dad and she said I better pray. And so that's why I was wondering if you could send her to The Phantom Zone instead of my brother Buster if that's OK with you? I hope I explained everything so you understand how importent it is, Superman. Thank you very much.

> Your Very Good Friends,
> JERRY AND ROBERT

PS: If you wanted to send both of them to The Phantom Zone then that would be OK too.

DEAR SUPERMAN,

I look at it this way. You're just as good as God and so I think it's OK if you're in his house and besides I know you wouldn't mind it if God was in your Fortress of Solitude. I just wanted to tell you that in case you felt bad about what Sister Mary Justin said. Robert helped me think of the idea to write and tell you that. So long.

> Your pals,
> Jerry Chariot and Robert

PS: I may not be able to write so much anymore because I don't get no allowence and can't buy no stamps nomore. Not since Sister Mary Justin called my dad and I got in all that trouble. But Robert said he would pay for all the stamps out of his allowence if we put his name first sometimes.

> Robert and Jerry Chariot

PS: Robert said to say HI to Jimmy Olsen if he isn't out getting a scoop.

DEAR SUPERPAL,

A lot of the kids in school have been laughing and teasing me about what happend in church the other day.

They even call me a SUPER SINNER and the way they talk about me is just like the way they talk about weather nunns have brests or not. Duane Machado who was Saint Joseph in the Christmas play said they don't have brests and it's just stuffed with pens and medals and roserys and stuff. Michael Roinski who was a sheep in the Christmas play said they do too have brests only they were cut down and made smaller just like nunns hair is cut short and everybody knows they're almost bald. And my bestfriend Robert said they have regular brests just like his mother's only they're not as big as his mother's who is also Italien like Robert is. So I thought maybe you could use your X-ray Vision to look under Sister Mary Justin's uniform and tell me if she's got brests or if it's other stuff? And then I could tell all the kids in school. And then maybe they'd like me and they wouldn't laugh at me and spit on me in the stairwell. Robert says Hello to you and Jimmy Olsen. Goodby.

>Your friends,
>JERRY CHARIOT AND ROBERT

PS: Me and Robert was climbing up to the Duck Rock which is way up in the hill behind my house and I thought I saw a meteor fall to the Earth and crash. So we tryed to find it because we thought it might be Kryptonite. Only we couldn't. That's why we thought as long as you're using your X-ray Vision on Sister Mary Justin maybe you could also find that Kryptonite. And then you could write us a letter and tell us where it is and we'll go get rid of it so it don't kill you in case you decide to come and visit us sometime. You're welcome.

Our Friend Superman,

Me and Robert just read THE PHANTOM SUPERBOY where you accidently got projected into The Phantom Zone in GIANT SUPERBOY NO. 165. It was too bad how that baby lizzerd accidently pressed the Black Button when you was standing in front of The Phantom Zone Punishment Machine and you disappeard. Boy, if that ever happend to me I would REALLY be scared but you never get sacred and that's why I like you so much. And so does Robert. And it's really hard to explain about what I wanted to explain about, Superman. But I'll try.

You see, Sister Mary Justin in school has been talking a lot about Purgatory lately and how that's where you go when you're not bad enough to suffer everlasting punishment in Hell and you're not good enough to suffer everlasting happiness in Heaven. She said you just have to wait there in Purgatory until God decides you sufferd a lot and then you get into Heaven. And if people on Earth pray for you while you're in Purgatory then you can get out sooner if you got enough prayers. Like about five hundred million Hail Marys.

But the only trouble is you're not allowed to pray for yourself while you're there because it's too late. That's why I'm praying a lot now in case I go to Purgatory when I die then I'll get out a LOT sooner. But if you go to Hell then it don't matter because you can NEVER get out of Hell. And that means you wasted a lot of time praying on Earth when you didn't have to. So far I have 677 Hail Marys and 12 Our Father Who Art In Heavens. Which is a LOT more than Robert.

Anyway, what me and Robert was thinking was that Purgatory and The Phantom Zone might be the exact same place exactly. Especially since you can get out of The Phantom Zone after a long time, just like you can get out of Purgatory after a long time. Except you don't have to pray to get out of The Phantom Zone. You just have to wait.

And me and Robert read in GIANT SUPERBOY NO. 165 how criminels on Krypton were sent to The Phantom Zone because then they were invisible and they couldn't steel nothing or kill nobody. And after they were there for a long time and they were sorry for their sins, then they could stand in front of The Phantom Zone Punishment Machine and somebody would press the White Button and they'd come back. That's the way it worked.

Well, Sister Mary Justin said God sends people to Purgatory just like you send people to The Phantom Zone only God doesn't have a Purgatory Machine. He just does it. And so Robert and me was thinking that if we ever go to Purgatory when we die then you could press the White Button and get us out. And then we wouldn't have to keep praying so much. And then we could write you more letters and maybe we could even start a Superman Fan Club. And I know this is very mixed up, but since you have Super branes we know you'll figure it out. Thank you very much.

> Your friend,
> JERRY and ROBERT SIPANNO

PS: Did you ever find that piece of Kryptonite and Sister Mary Justin's brests?

DEAR SUPERMAN,

The other day Robert said maybe Superman was really God and I laughed. He said maybe Superman is really God just like Clark Kent is really Superman because you and God both can send people to Purgatory. I told Robert I would write and ask you just in case he might be right. So could you please tell us if you're really God and if Superman is just your secret identity and we promise we won't tell anybody else? Not even anybody who might join our Superfan Club when we start it. Thank you.

Your friend,
JERRY CHARIOT

PS: If you're God then me and Robert will pray a lot more but we'll still write letters.

———— ✂ ————

Dear Man of Steel,

I hope you don't mind if I put two letters in one envelope but I just figured something out and so I told Robert and so now we don't think you're God anymore. I told Robert that The Phantom Zone and Purgatory can't be the same place since when people get out of The Phantom Zone they come back to Earth and they don't go to Heaven. And so if you can't send people to Heaven then you can't be God. Robert said he had to think about it because he had a funny feeling you're still God. But even if you're not, we still hope you'll press the White Button and get us out of Purgatory if we happen to go there. Thank you very much again.

YOUR PALS,
Jerry and Robert

PS: Remember that Superfan Club I was telling you about? Well, I think I should be President but Robert don't. He thinks he should be President. And so we decided that you should decide. We both think we would be good Presidents except I think I would be better. So could you hurry up and tell us so we'll know? Thank you.

DEAR CLARK KENT, if you know what I mean,

Me and Robert know a lot about you but we won't say it here in case somebody picks this up off your desk or something and guesses what you don't want them to guess. Especially Lois Lane who thinks you're Superman—isn't that dumb Ha-Ha! (I put that in just in case.) Anyway, the reason we're sending this letter to you is because we know you see Superman sometimes and we want you to tell him something for us the next time you see him which might be any minute if you know what I mean. Tell him we found that Kryptonite meteor which wasn't really Kryptonite but we burried it anyway just in case there was Kryptonite inside of it. So now he don't have to worry if he flies over the Duck Rock where me and Robert have our new Secret Hiding Place ever since Old Lady Holbrook caught us in our old one and told my dad. The Duck Rock is a lot better anyway because it's REAL big and it sticks WAY up in the air and if you fell off the top you'd probly get killed unless you knew how to fly. Which I don't yet. Which is why my mom said I was NEVER allowed to climb up on top and neither is any of the other kids and that's why me and Robert picked it. Because everybody else is chicken to climb on the Duck. And because it's a real good spot to land on. And because it's real easy to find especially if you got X-ray Vision. Which reminds me. Would you also tell Superman that it don't matter if he looks at Sister Mary Justin's brests or not because Robert asked his older brother Bruno if nunns have brests and Bruno said if she didn't have brests then she would be a priest. But tell Superman we said thank you for trying very much anyway.

Sincerly Yours,
JERRY CHARIOT and ROBERT SIPANNO

Dear SUPERMAN,

Every time I pick up one of your books I see Lois Lane is trying to bother you by trying to figure out your Secret Identity and I don't know why you still like her so much. I mean Jimmy Olsen doesn't do things like sneaking up from behind and trying to cut your hair to see if the sizzors will break because your hair is indestructable like everything else you have. I know Lois worships the ground you fly over and she even wants to merry you but if she REALLY loved you then she wouldn't bother you so much and she would just love you whoever you are like me and Robert do. Doesn't she know that if everybody knew you was really Clark Kent then everybody would want to come and see you and go for a ride on your back and bother you all the time? And then you wouldn't have time to get scoops or save people or play with your Superdog Krypto. Me and Robert was thinking maybe we should write Lois a letter and tell her not to be so nosey. But we thought we should ask you first so what do you think?

Love,
JERRY and ROBERT

PS: Do you really think you might get merried to Lois Lane someday? Or are you waiting to see if maybe you could find a girl with Super powers like your cousin Supergirl who you can't merry because she's your cousin? My mother said that Negro people shouldn't merry anybody else except other Negro people, just like Catholics are only allowed to merry Catholics and nobody should ever merry a Jew. Not even the Protestents. So me and Robert decided that if my mom believed in you then she'd want you to merry somebody who's Super instead of normel. But she don't anyway and neither does my dad or Buster or Sister Mary Justin. So me and Robert thought about it for a LONG time and we decided you should merry ANYBODY you want to. Except maybe Lois Lane. And then if you married somebody who's normel then maybe I could merry somebody who's not normel like your cousin Supergirl. I love Supergirl a HOLE LOT even almost as much as I love you, Superman. So long.

JERRY AGAIN

PS: By the way, is Supergirl a Catholic?

Dear SUPERFRIEND,

Yesterday I started to write you a letter and tell you how I would be a better President than Robert because I'm learning how to fly and be just like you and that's why I practice every day unless Old Lady Holbrook is around. But then Robert came in and he saw me writing it and he got REAL mad because it was the first time I ever wrote a letter without him. And he wouldn't talk to me and he wouldn't let me read the latest SUPERMAN'S PAL JIMMY

OLSEN or anything. And today in school when we went to the lavatory he wouldn't even whisper to me like he usually does when Sister Mary Justin's outside waiting. He just looked at his thing and I just looked at my thing and we didn't say anything. And so after school I decided to tell him how he could be President if he wants. Only he said we shouldn't have a President or a Vice President or anything because we'll just have us. And this way we'll NEVER have to fight anymore unless we want to. And so now you don't have to worry about which one you're gonna pick anymore. We know you was having a hard time deciding and that's why you took so long because you like both of us a lot. So do we. So goodby.

Your Superfans,
JERRY and ROBERT

Dear Lois Lane,

We used to think Clark Kent was Superman but now we don't anymore. You see, last week we saw Clark Kent standing on the corner innerviewing somebody for a scoop when allofasudden Superman went flying up near the Duck Rock. So he can't be two places at once like God can. So you see, he isn't.

Goodby.

Sincerly,
Mr. Chariot and Mr. Sipanno

Dear SUPERMAN,

We usually have Religion first in the morning but

sometimes we have it last and we have Geography first. And sometimes we don't have Geography at all because Sister Mary Justin thinks it's better we should know about where we're going after we die than where we're going now. So the other morning during Geography class Sister Mary Justin asked us where we would like to go most of all if we could go ANYWHERE in the hole world most of all. That's what she said, the hole world, and so I couldn't say Krypton or Mars. And I was the first one who raised my hand but she still called on Jimmy Sinceri first. She always calls on Jimmy Sinceri first because his older brother is a alter boy and so she likes him. It don't matter that I have a older sister who is becoming a nunn because that don't count because of what happend in church which I already told you about. But I never told you about my sister the Sister because I don't like her very much sometimes. Because every time we get to go see her she always tells me how Sister Mary Justin is one of the BEST nunns in the HOLE convent and how I'm REALLY lucky to have her. The only trouble is that Sister Mary Justin likes certain people and she don't like certain people and if you're one of the ones she don't like then she really HATES you. Because that's the way nunns are.

Anyway, the other day in Geography class Jimmy Sinceri said he wanted to go to Heaven more than anywhere else in the hole world. But since he couldn't go to Heaven until after he dies then he'd like to go to Roam where the Pope lives. And Sister Mary Justin liked that.

And then Janie Jobb said she'd like to go to Jeruslum because that's where Jesus died and she'd like to go walk where Jesus walked on the day he died which was Good Friday last year. And Sister Mary Justin liked that also.

And then Jane Barroni raised her hand and said she wanted to go to the bathroom and she went.

And then Sister Mary Justin said JEROME? And I knew the way she said my real name that she wasn't gonna like what I said even if I didn't tell the truth. So I told the truth.

And she said METROPOLIS? I NEVER HEARD OF IT. And I said That's where Superman lives. And she said SUPERMAN! And I should have known right then to be quiet but I didn't. And so I said Yes, I want to go to Metropolis so I can see Superman and talk to him and maybe even touch him and shake his hand. And that's when Sister Mary Justin started to laugh only she didn't really laugh because it was one of those laughs which says BOY ARE YOU STUPID! And when she laughs like that, that means everybody else in the class is supposed to laugh too. And so they do. And if they don't then they might get in trouble like I was. Only I think they really like to laugh like that. Especially Jimmy Sinceri.

And so Sister Mary Justin said WHERE IS METROPOLIS, JEROME? And I really hate Jerome even if Saint Jerome was one of the BEST saints in the hole church. But I guess Saint Jerry wouldn't sound very good. So I said It's in Pencilvania. And she said WHERE? Only she said it like she already knew. And I said It's in Pencilvania again. And she didn't say anything for a long time and she kept looking at me. And then she said WILL YOU PLEASE GO TO THE BLACKBOARD? And so I went. And she said PULL DOWN THE MAP OF PENCILVANIA. And I said I can't reach it. And she said DUANE? And so Duane did it. And then she said FIND IT! and so I looked.

That's when she took her watch out from under where she keeps her brests and things and she looked at it. And I looked at the map. Only it was hard to see because my eyes were all watery because everybody was giggling at me.

And then she started tapping her foot like she does when a test is almost over and she wants to make you nervous. And I was.

And she said WELL? And I said I can't find it. And she said OF COURSE YOU CAN'T FIND IT! And I said Maybe it's somewhere else. Maybe it's in New York or Ohio? And she said YOU ARE SO STUPID! I DON'T KNOW HOW YOU COULD HAVE A SISTER WHO IS BECOMING A NUNN! And I said Maybe it's in Californya? And she said IT ISN'T ANYWHERE, JEROME! THERE IS NO METROPOLIS JUST LIKE THERE IS NO SUPERMAN! YOU CAN LOOK ALL DAY AND YOU WILL NEVER FIND IT! NEVER! And I said Yes I will! And she said NO YOU WON'T! And I said YES I WILL! again.

That's when she started to get REALLY mad, Superman. She said I had to do extra homework because I was so dumb and she said I had to write five hundred times THERE IS NO SUPERMAN and she said my mom and dad had to sign it. And you know what I figured, Superman? I figured if I did that then I wouldn't only be dumb but I'd be a dumb lier. So I said No. And she said WHAT DID YOU JUST SAY TO ME? And I was really crying and I was really scared but I said NO I WON'T DO IT! THERE IS TOO A SUPERMAN AND I AIN'T GONNA BE A LIER! I AIN'T GONNA GO TO HELL FOR YOU BECAUSE SOMEDAY HE'S GONNA FLY IN HERE THROUGH THE WINDOW AND THEN YOU'LL FIND OUT AND THEN YOU'LL BE SORRY!

Well let me tell you, Superman, she didn't like that at all. She walked right over to me and she hit me right across the face and she grabbed me by the ear and she dragged me out of the classroom and nobody was laughing anymore because even Jimmy Sinceri was afraid. And she dragged me down the steps and into the boys lavatory and it's a good thing nobody was peeing inside because she didn't even knock first. She just grabbed some sope and she put it to my mouth and she said CHEW!

And I said NO!

And she said CHEW IT, JEROME!

And I turned my head away.

And she grabbed my chin and squeezd it real hard and she pushed the sope in and I tried to spit it out and so she hit me across the face again.

TALKING TO A NUNN LIKE THAT! she said. I CAN'T BELIEVE IT! I JUST CAN'T BELIEVE IT!

And my ear was hurting and my face was hurting and my mouth was hurting and I was starting to feel sick. Real sick. In my stomick. And before I knew it all my Rice Krispies and bananas came up and went allover her robes and beads and stuff. And so she got madder and I got sicker and she hit me again. And then she took me up to Sister Agnes Therese the Principle. And then Sister Agnes Therese called my dad and when he took me home he got out the strap and it still hurts. And my dad said THAT'S NOTHING COMPARED TO WHAT YOU'RE GONNA GET IF I EVER CATCH YOU READING ANOTHER SUPERMAN COMICBOOK OR IF I EVER HEAR YOU SAY THE NAME SUPERMAN AGAIN OR IF I EVER TALK BACK TO A NUNN!

And that's the main reason I'm writing this letter, Superman. I thought I should let you know that if you ever decide to write back and tell me where Metropolis is then maybe you should send it to Robert's house and he'll give it to me OK?

Thank you very very very verymuch.

Your Friend,
JERRY CHARIOT

PS: Robert's address is: 155 Elk Avenue
Pulpburg, Pencilvania

———⛓———

Dear Lois Lane,

My name is Mrs. Holbrook and I have a daughter who looks just like you only she isn't as pretty. And she used to think that Clark Kent and Superman was the Same person. But then she saw them walking into Holy Redeemer Church together and so now she don't. So there.

Yours Truely,
Mrs. O. L. Holbrook

———⛓———

Dear SUPERMAN,

I'm sorry we haven't written you a letter in such a long time but me and Robert have been too busy looking for Metropolis in the library where we didn't find it yet. But don't worry because we will. We decided we would get a map of every state and check every dot because we gotta find it so Robert can tell Sister Mary Justin where it's at. Because it wouldn't be a good idea if I was the one who told her because she won't listen to me anyway. Anyway, we already checked all the A's and B's and C's and Deleware and it isn't there. And it probly isn't in Florida because we ain't never seen no palm trees in Metropolis. And it probly isn't in Georgia because we ain't never seen no Negros either. It sure would help if you just wrote us a letter and told us which state it was in but we know how you're too busy saving people all the time. Besides, if I'm ever gonna develop my brane and make it Super like yours then I

31

better get started right away and figure it out all by myself and Robert. So thank you.

PS: Pretty soon you won't have to worry about Lois Lane bothering you anymore and trying to guess your Secret Identity. We're taking care of her.

Dear Superpal,

I started to write a letter to your cousin Supergirl but then I changed my mind because I thought maybe you could tell her for me. Thanks. It isn't that I don't think she's pretty because I think she's pretty pretty. And she's got the exact same Super powers that you've got and I'm getting. Except she's a girl and so she can't be as strong as you, Superman. But she's still stronger than any other normel people (even men) and so I thought I better not merry her until I get Super also. If I do. Someday.

You see, Superman, I don't think I'd like a wife who's stronger than me and so everybody would say she has to protect me. My dad says he's the king in his own castle because he's a man and a man is the king in his own castle. He says that a lot. Except we don't really have a castle because it's just a apartment building. But my dad is still king of the apartment building along with all the other kings in all the other apartments. And that's what I want to be. But that's what I wouldn't be if Supergirl fought all the crime in the family. Do you understand? The other day I jumped out of Old Lady Holbrook's apple tree again and I flew even farther than the last time and you can even ask

Robert again if you want to. And so it shouldn't be very long now. So I hope you'll tell her, Man of Steel. Thank you.

YOUR PAL,
JERRY

PS: We checked the E's and the F's and the G's and Hawaii and it isn't there. And since everybody in Metropolis speaks English then it must be in America huh? It's not in England is it? They speak English there also you know.

GOSH, SUPERMAN,

We just read ACTION COMICS NO. 368 and Robert hated it almost as much as I did and I REALLY hated it. It was the AWFULEST adventure you ever had, even awfuller than the time you got changed into a giant ant after you got exposed to some Red Kryptonite when you was trying to save the world from doom. You know, sometimes I think that Red Kryptonite is even worse than Green Kryptonite but none of them's as bad as Gold Kryptonite which can take away all your Super powers and make you just ordinary but not dead.

Anyway, in ACTION COMICS NO. 368 I really HATED how there was no more crime in the world and everybody was good and so the policemen had no more work to do except help little kids across the street. And it was TERRIBLE how there was no more disasters in the world and so you didn't have any lifes to save. And you didn't have any floods to throw back. And so the world didn't need Superman nomore.

It was REALLY bad on page one where all the policemen was playing checkers and the captin said, "Nobody's so much as jaywalked for a month, Superman! Half my officers and detectives are counting stolen loot that criminels voluntarily turned in!" And so you looked at him and said, "GREAT KRYPTON!" And then you said, "Earth is now a crimeless, warless, trouble-free world! And I fit in like a vegetarian at a steak barbecue!"

And you know what, Superman? I wanted to CRY because things were so bad! That's why I'm glad it didn't last long because then nobody would need you anymore except me and Robert because we'll ALWAYS need you. And if there wasn't nomore crimes then there wouldn't be nomore sins and then the priests wouldn't have a job either and then nobody would believe in you or God or nothing. They'd just believe in themselves.

So me and Robert wanted to let you know we don't hate Luthor or Mr. Mxyzptlk! so much anymore even if they are REALLY bad. I hope you understand. What we're trying to say is you shouldn't chase too many criminels too quick. And if you do then maybe it'd be a good idea if you let a couple of them excape every once in a while. Because if people didn't be so BAD then you wouldn't be so GOOD and so I hope you understand.

Thank you, Mr. Crimefighter!

> Your VERY good friends,
> JERRY and ROBERT

PS: I hope you don't think we like criminels or anything like that. We still hate them. Only we don't really hate them. So long, Man of Steel.

Dear LOIS LANE,

I am the Lord thy God and thou shalt not think that Clark Kent is thy Superman. Amen.

Yours truely,
God the Father Almighty
Heaven, U.S.A.

Dear SUPERMAN,

Well you don't have to worry about Lois Lane anymore for a while. You're welcome.

JERRY and ROBERT SIPANNO

The
Second
Dimension

Dear Superman,

WE FOUND IT! WE FOUND IT! We found it in World Book Encyclopedia VOL. 9 under Illinoise which is where it's at! GOSH, Superman, I'm happy! I'm REALLLLLLLLLLLY happy! And so is my friend Robert. On the map it says that Metropolis is about 37 degrees North and 80 degrees West and the dot isn't as big as I expected but it isn't as small as some of them. BOY OH BOY OH BOY, SUPERMAN! I knew all along I'd find it. I KNEW it! Robert wasn't so sure because when we got to Hawaii he said maybe we should stop for a while but I said NO! See, I told you. I AM getting Super branes! Aren't you glad? Goodby.

ALMOST SUPER-JERRY

(and Robert too)

PS: As soon as we get a chance, Robert's gonna tell Sister Mary Justin where it's at. Boy I can't wait to see her face when we tell her!

Dear Superman again,

I know I wrote you a letter last night but I just HAD to write to you again today and let you know again how REALLY glad I was that we found it in Illinoise. I'm even gladder than I've ever been in my entire hole life. Of course when I develop ALL my Super powers and get to fly to Metropolis, Illinoise, then that'll be the gladdest moment I ever had. But until then right now is my gladdest entire moment and that's why I wanted to say Thank You Thank You Thank You Thank YouThankYouThank You Thank YOU thank YOU thank YOU thank YOU THANK YOU THANK YOU THANK YOU THANK YOU THANK YOU VERY MUCH!

I LOVE YOU, SUPER PAL!

Jerry Chariot

━━━━◁◈▷━━━━

Dear SUPERman,

We're supposed to be starting our Religion homework now but I just HAD to write you a letter right away and tell you about the dream I had which is VERY importent because it might save your life from death.

You see, Superman, last night I drempt that somebody gave you a gold coin which is JUST like the one my Ant Hellen has which is real old and real gold. And she said she's gonna give it to me someday when I grow up when she dies. That's why I always have to kiss her every time we go visit her and Uncle Dominic every Sunday. Except I don't like to kiss her mouth because it's all wrinkled and ugly but I do it anyway especially when she lets me look at that gold coin she's gonna give me if I keep on kissing her. So I do.

Only the coin I dreamed about wasn't real gold because it was Gold Kryptonite and it took away ALL your Super powers, Superman. And that's when you saw this woman with a baby going across the street and a truck was coming and the truck didn't have any breaks and so you ran into a phone booth in front of Andy's Donuts and turned into

Superman. Only you didn't know you wasn't Super nomore. And so you jumped right in front of the truck and you put out your hands and yelled,

"THIS IS A JOB . . . FOR SUPERMAN!"

Which is when the truck ran over you and the mother and the baby too. And then it ran right into Bacchio's News Stand and it killed Mrs. Bacchio when she was standing behind the counter where I always buy my comicbooks every Monday after school when Mr. Durrelli brings them in at 4 o'clock. And that's why I thought I should tell you about that dream RIGHT away so you can be REAL careful in case Mr. Mxyzptlk! or somebody gives you a gold coin. Goodby.

YOUR FRIEND JERRY CHARIOT

———

SUPERPAL,

My mom said sometimes dreams come true. Like the time she dreamed that Mrs. Fazzari up the street was dieing and two weeks later she died of a hard attack. She was 91 years old. And every time one of the neighbors dies then my mom bakes apple pies and cakes and stuff like that and she brings them to the house where the body used to live and where all the relatives are crying and eating. I remember how I had to kneel in front of Mrs. Fazzari's dead body and say a prayer so her soul wouldn't go to Hell and I couldn't have any pie until I did it. And so I did it. And that's when I noticed that her lips were real red and she had a nice smile which I never saw before. And her dress was real pretty and she looked a LOT better than she ever did in real life. So I was thinking maybe death isn't

41

such a bad thing after all but still I hope you'll be REAL careful around any gold, Superman. Because if you do touch any, then don't forget to make sure you have ALL your Super powers before you stand in front of any trucks that don't have any breaks OK? Goodby again.

JERRY again

PS: Robert didn't get a chance to tell Sister Mary Justin about Metropolis yet because we haven't had Geography for three days because we had three extra Religion classes instead because we're gonna be making our First Holy Communion pretty soon. But don't worry, he'll tell her. Because if he don't then I will.

———⚬———

Dear Man of Tomorrow,

The other day in Geography class Sister Mary Justin was talking about the Holy Trinity. And she said there's three persons in one God and they're the Father and the Son and the Holy Ghost amen. And I said HOW CAN THERE BE THREE PERSONS WHEN THERE ISN'T EVEN ONE PERSON BECAUSE HE'S A GOD AND NOT A PERSON? And Sister Mary Justin said THAT'S TRUE, HE IS A GOD BUT THERE ARE THREE DIFFERENT PARTS TO THAT GOD. And I said YOU MEAN LIKE A PUZZEL? And Sister Mary Justin said NOT EXACTLY, IT'S MORE LIKE A STATUE WITH THREE FACES. And I said HOW DO YOU KNOW GOD HAS THREE FACES IF YOU CAN'T SEE HIM UNTIL AFTER YOU DIE LIKE YOU TOLD US? And Sister Mary Justin was starting to get mad. But she said WELL, GOD TOLD US. And I said WHO DID HE TELL? And she

42

said THE WORLD. And I said WHEN? And she said WHEN HIS ONLY SON JESUS CHRIST CAME DOWN ON EARTH AND DIED FOR OUR SINS. And I said HOW DID JESUS KNOW? And she said BECAUSE HE'S THE SON OF GOD AND SO HE'S A MEMBER OF THE HOLY TRINITY AND SO HE'S REALLY GOD AND SO HE KNOWS EVERY-THING. And I said I STILL DON'T GET IT. And Sister Mary Justin said YOU SHOULD NOT BE A DOUBTING THOM-AS. SIT DOWN, JEROME! So I sat down.

So after school Robert and me talked about it a long time and we decided that it's easy to see how sometimes you can be SUPERMAN and sometimes you can be CLARK KENT. But you can never be both at the same time. So how can Sister Mary Justin believe in three Gods that you can never see until after you die but she don't believe in one Superman that you can watch on TV? That's what we can't figure out. Maybe she's been praying too much and God's been giving her too much information and she's getting it all mixed up. That's what I said. So Robert said WELL, MAYBE I BETTER NOT TELL HER ABOUT METROPOLIS BECAUSE SHE'LL JUST GET THAT MIXED UP TOO AND I'LL GET IN TROUBLE. And I said YOU'RE JUST ASCARED TO TELL HER BECAUSE YOU'RE CHICKEN! And Robert said NO SIR I AM NOT! So I started making noises like a chicken. And so now Robert's gonna tell her if we ever have Geography again.

> Your friends,
> JERRY and ROBERT SIPANNO

Dear Superman,

Well, we had Geography again and Robert said I better

not write and tell you about it because it was REALLY terrible and Robert cried like I did. But I said we have to tell Superman because he's our friend and we told him we would. My mom says a friend is a person who you can tell bad things to and they'll listen. And I said I thought that's what a priest was? And my mom said Yes, a priest is also a friend. But Robert said if I tell you about it then he'll NEVER speak to me again in his hole life and maybe even longer. Like if we both go to the same place like Heaven or Hell or Purgatory. And you know what I think, Superman? I think he means it. In fact I'm sure he does. And so I'm really sorry. I hope you understand and don't get mad or anything. You see, Robert is also my friend and I don't have too many friends anymore and I really like Robert quite a bit. And so I better not tell you OK? Because I know Robert would REALLY feel bad if I told you how everybody laughed at him and called him names and how Sister Mary Justin said he was almost as dumb as Jerome if that's possible. And he would feel even badder if you told Jimmy Olsen about it. So I better not do it because I just can't. So I hope you really understand.

YOUR FRIEND,
JERRY

PS: GOSH you shoulda seen it, Superman!

———————

DEAR SUPERMAN,

I just read that story about you and Mr. Mxyzptlk! and I think he's really neat. I like him better than anybody I ever read about in your comicbooks except for you and

44

Supergirl and Jimmy Olsen. And Robert likes him quite a bit too. And that's why we're writing this letter.

You see, Superman, we don't think Mr. Mxyzptlk! is really that bad even if he does make a lot of trouble for you and everybody else in Metropolis, Illinoise. Especially you. Because he does those things to have fun and not to hurt people or kill somebody. Because he isn't real big and mean like Luthor is. In fact he's about as little—I mean big—as I and Robert am. That's why he's a imp and not a person. He doesn't do things like robbing banks or pushing Lois Lane out the window. He just does things like making cars drive up the side of skyscrapers and making all the water disappear from the swimming pool. He likes to make trouble because that's just the way he is, not because he really LIKES to make trouble.

And we think it's really NEAT how he comes out of The Fifth Dimension where he lives with all the the other imps, and the only way you can send him back to his own Dimension is to make him spell his name backwords. And that's the only way you can get rid of him because he's magical and you can't catch him. Because every time you try and grab him somebody writes POP! and he's gone, just like that! He's pretty smart. That's why you can never trick him until the last page of the comicbook.

I remember one time you tricked him by making him read the letters in his alphabet soup which turned out to be his name spelt backwords. I thought that was REALLY clever. That's something I would of thought of. You're really great, Superman! And Mr. Mxyzptlk! isn't so bad as you think sometimes. Because EVERYbody likes to do tricks like that. Even me. Like one time I hid in the apple tree and waited for my cousin Connie to walk under and then I peed on her. The reason I did it was because she always told my mom when I ran behind her house and pulled my pants down in front of cars going by. And another time I put a frog down Robert's pants but I can't do things like making cars drive up the side of Holy Redeemer School or turning Sister Mary Justin into a wart. So you don't have to worry.

And since Mr. Mxyzptlk! keeps coming back to this Dimension every 90 days I guess you'll be busy enough trying to trick him and making him spell his name backwords. And so me and Robert are gonna help you OK? And our first idea is to pretend you are a blind person and you can even dress up like one with sun glasses and everything. And Mr. Mxyzptlk! won't know it's really you and so you could ask him to read you a story out of a old comicbook. And you could pick one where you already tricked him into spelling his name backwords. And then when he got to the end he'd disappear. Isn't that good Ha-Ha?

> Your PALS,
> Jerry and Robert

PS: If you don't like that one then we'll send you another one as soon as we think of it. Which should be pretty soon, so don't worry.

Dear Superman,

Robert said to tell you that he didn't really cry very much because Sister Mary Justin only hit him once. And besides it made some more freckles grow when the tears fell allover his face and so now he REALLY looks like

Jimmy Olsen a hole lot. In fact we was thinking of taking Robert's picture and sending it to Jimmy Olsen so Jimmy Olsen would open it and say GREAT KRYPTON! HE MUST BE MY TWIN BROTHER! And then maybe Jimmy Olsen might want to meet Robert and so he might ask you to fly him here to Pulpburg. And if you wanted to stay over night then Jimmy could stay with Robert and you could stay at my house because I don't think my mom would mind too much once she gets a chance to meet you. So what do you think?

ROBERT'S FRIEND,
JERRY

—✦—

Dear SUPERMAN,

Me and Robert have been thinking about it and we decided that maybe you and God really should get to meet each other sometime. You see, Sister Mary Justin says God can see everything that's going on in the world and so can you if you use your X-ray Vision. And Sister Mary Justin says God can be everywhere at once and so can you if you use your Super-speed. I mean, you can go all the way to Mars in only two seconds and that's pretty god. I mean good. And Sister Mary Justin also says that nothing can kill God except the Jews and all that can kill you is Kryptonite. And that can't be much worse than the Jews. And just think, some day you might invent a cure for Kryptonite but how can you invent a cure for the Jews?

Of course I never saw a real Jew because we don't have any here in Pulpburg. We just have Catholics and Italiens and Pollacks and Protestents. And every time my dad comes in from work my mom says YOU'RE DIRTY AS A NIGGER! And so one time when we went to visit my Ant Emma on the train in Buffalo I pointed at the conductor and yelled LOOK, MOM! HE'S DIRTY AS A NIGGER LIKE DAD! And my mom got all red and she said NOW HOW MANY TIMES HAVE I TOLD YOU TO CALL THEM NE- GROS, JERRY? And I said YOU AIN'T NEVER TOLD ME! And my mom looked at me just like Sister Mary Justin looks at me. That's when I learned you're supposed to call them Negros when you talk in front of them but you can call them Niggers when my dad comes home from work. I think it would be a lot easier if you just called them one thing and then you wouldn't have to worry about it all the time. But I don't think anybody else around here thinks like I think you're supposed to think like.

You see, Superpal, Pulpburg is a pretty small place and everybody knows who you are except they call you by your dad's name instead of your own. And since my dad's name is Anthony they all call me Little Tony. Or else they call me Little Buster which is even worse. Or else they don't even pay any attention to me which is what usually happens. Except when I do something like spitting from the upstairs porch and trying to make it land in the mailman's pouch when he looked up and I got it on his nose. And then my dad paid a LOT of attention to me.

Anyway, my mom says God talks to nunns and I hope you don't do that also, Superman. Because you dress a lot better and you're a lot handsomer and I think your red boots are a LOT nicer than sandels. So I hope you don't ever decide to grow a beard.

The thing I don't like about God is how he got murderd by the Jews which is who I was telling you about before the Negros. He couldn't find a way to excape before they grabbed him and nailed him to a cross in the end. Which wasn't really the end because he came alive again. Which is pretty good. But I think it would be a lot better if he just got away in the beginning like you got away from Krypton. Maybe what he needed is Super branes like you and me are gonna have except you already have them.

Which just gave me a good idea, Superman.

What you could do is fly faster than the speed of light and crash through the Time Barrier. And you could land in Jeruslum just when they're gonna nail him to that cross. And you could fly down and all the guards would try to stab you with their speers and their speers would break on your chest and you'd just laugh and say HA-HA IT TICKELS! And then you'd grab Jesus and fly away with him to a safe hiding place like maybe the Duck Rock. And then it would say THE END. And then me and Robert could take the comicbook to school and show Sister Mary Justin. Boy would she be surprised!

LOVE,
Jerry and Robert

DEAR SUPER FRIEND,

After school me and Robert was in Bacchio's News Stand waiting for Mr. Durrelli to bring the latest SUPERMAN'S PAL JIMMY OLSEN and he was late. And we was really getting worried because maybe he had a accident or something and maybe his truck started on fire and maybe the latest SUPERMAN'S PAL JIMMY OLSEN NO. whatever it was gonna be got all burned up or something. And that would be really awful because then we'd have to wait until they got more in and what if they NEVER got any more in? It was almost four thirdy and that's why we was so worried because I had to be home by five to dump the garbage and so did Robert. We always have to do things like that and the dishes which I REALLY hate. And if he didn't come pretty soon then we'd have to wait until tomorrow and I wouldn't be able to sleep tonight because that's what happened once before when it snowed a hole lot and Mr. Durrelli's truck got stuck on Shawmut Avenue and he never got there in time. It was awful. But it wasn't snowing today and it wasn't even raining and that's why we was so worried. And Mrs. Bacchio kept looking at us looking worried. And it was going on five o'clock and Mr. Durrelli still didn't come and Mrs. Bacchio was still looking at us and she was smiling. And then she said MY, YOU BOYS MUST SURE LIKE COMICBOOKS.

And Robert said WE SURE DO.

And I said YOU SEE MRS. BACCHIO, WE DON'T REALLY LIKE COMICBOOKS. WE JUST LIKE SUPERMAN AND SUPERGIRL AND SUPERDOG AND JIMMY OLSEN. THAT'S ALL. EXCEPT WE ALSO LIKE SUPERHORSE AND PERRY WHITE AND MA AND PA KENT.

And Robert said WE SURE DO.

And I said YOU SEE, WE DON'T LIKE DONALD DUCK AND LITTLE LULU BECAUSE THEY'RE FOR KIDS AND NOT US. AND BESIDES THEY DON'T FLY OR NOTHING.

And Robert said THEY SURE DON'T.

And I said WE DON'T MIND BATMAN AND WONDER WOMAN AND GREEN LANTERN AND FLASH AND PEOPLE LIKE THAT. BUT YOU SEE, WE DON'T HAVE VERY MUCH MONEY AND SO WE LIKE SUPERMAN THE BEST. THAT'S BECAUSE HE IS THE BEST.

And that's when Mrs. Bacchio laughed and said YOU

KNOW, I KINDA LIKE SUPERMAN MYSELF. And the reason I'm putting in all these BIG letters is so you can tell who's talking easier. You're welcome.

And she's the first big person we ever met who likes Superman, Superman. So I didn't trust her. And neither did Robert. So I said OK, IF YOU LIKE SUPERMAN THEN YOU MUST KNOW WHAT CAN KILL HIM. SO WHAT IS IT?

And she said JUST ONE THING. KRYPTONITE.

And Robert said HEY, SHE DOES KNOW!

And I said WELL LOTS OF PEOPLE KNOW THAT. So I turned to Mrs. Bacchio and I looked at her for a long time right in her eyes. And I said OK, IF YOU'RE SO SMART THEN TELL ME WHAT SUPERMAN'S REAL NAME IS?

And she said YOU MEAN CLARK KENT?

And I said NO, I MEAN HIS REAL NAME ON KRYP-TON THAT HIS REAL MOM AND DAD GAVE HIM BE-FORE KRYPTON BLEW UP AND HE CAME TO EARTH IN A ROCKET TO BECOME SUPERBABY AND SOMEDAY SUPERMAN?

And she said THAT'S EASY.

And I said THEN WHAT IS IT?

And she said HIS REAL NAME WAS KAL-EL. AND HIS REAL FATHER'S NAME WAS JOR-EL. AND HIS REAL MOTHER'S NAME WAS LARA.

And Robert said GOSH!

But I didn't say nothing because I still didn't trust her. So I asked her a bunch of other questions like HOW DO YOU GET RID OF MR. MXYZPTLK!? And she said MR. WHO? And I said MR. MXYZPTLK! And she said OH, I THOUGHT IT WAS PRONOUNCED MXYZPTLK! And I said WELL ME AND ROBERT SAY MXYZPTLK! And so she told us.

She knew the answers to EVERYTHING, Superman.

And she kept smiling at us. And she smiled real nice, just like all the saints on the Holy Cards smile when they look up toward Heaven and a light shines on them. So me and Robert liked her a HOLE LOT. We really really did. We liked her more than any other groan ups we ever met, even the ones we have to like. Like my Ant Hellen who I don't really like anyway.

And that's why we hope you're REALLLLLLLLLLY careful if anybody gives you a gold coin OK? Because now you have to make SURE to save Mrs. Bacchio from that truck that I told you about. I was gonna tell Mrs. Bacchio about that dream, but then I figured I better not because she might get worried like me and Robert was worried about Mr. Durrelli. But then he came in at the last minute Thank God with the comicbooks. So we buyed SUPERMAN'S PAL JIMMY OLSEN and you know what she did? She gave us GIANT SUPERBOY NO. 17 free.

FREE!

So we said THANK YOU MRS. BACCHIO and she said YOU'RE WELCOME BOYS and we ran all the way home and dumped the garbage. And then I sneaked upstairs and started writing you this letter. And pretty soon we're gonna eat supper. And then I'm going up to Robert's house and we're gonna do our homework after we read the comicbooks. After I write you another letter.

So goodby for now.

> Your friends,
> JERRY and ROBERT

PS: Does Mrs. Bacchio ever write you letters?

DEAR SUPERMAN,

If you want to know why this letter smells like liver that's because I didn't wash my hands after supper because I was in a hurry to read the story called THE PUNISH-MENT OF SUPERBOY and so I hope you like liver. Especially since you got Super-smell. Boy Superman, I sure liked the way you talked back to Pa Kent when he wouldn't let you chop the wood with Super-speed. I thought that was REAL dumb. If I was Super then I wouldn't want to do anything regular either. So I was glad when you told Pa Kent, BUT I WON'T CHOP THAT WOOD LIKE AN ORDI-NARY BOY. IT'S A WASTE OF MY TIME!

And Pa Kent said, STILL DISOBEDIENT, EH? INTO THE WOODSHED, YOUNG MAN! YOU MUST BE PUN-ISHED!

And so he grabbed your ear and he took you in and he put you over his knee and he hit you just like my dad always hits me. Which is real hard. Except he forgot you're invulnerable. And so he said,

THIS WILL HURT ME MORE THAN . . . OWWWW! and he broke his hand. And that's why I can't wait till I become indestructable, Superman. This way when my dad hits me like that then he'll also break his hand too. And I'll laugh and say, I'M INDESTRUCTABLE, DAD! HA-HA!

And so he'll say, THEN YOU HAVE TO GO TO BED EARLY WITHOUT WATCHING I LOVE LUCY WHICH IS MY FAVORITEST PROGRAM EXCEPT FOR SUPERMAN. And I'll say,

THAT'S OK DAD, BECAUSE I CAN SEE THE TELEVI-SION WITH MY X-RAY VISION ANYWAY. AND I CAN HEAR IT WITH MY SUPER-HEARING. SO GOODNIGHT, DAD. HA-HA!

And so my dad will say, YOU AIN'T GETTING NO

MORE ALLOWENCE, YOUNG MAN! I'LL TEACH YOU!

And so I'll go down in the celler and I'll get a piece of coal and I'll press it into a diamond with the Super-strength of my Super hand. And then I'll fly it down to Nelson Jewlers and sell it for 20 DOLLERS! Which is a LOT more than my real allowence. And I'll show him just like you showed Pa Kent! He couldn't punish you because you was SUPERBOY and he was just a ordinary human person. And so he finally said,

I CAN'T HANDLE CLARK AND IT'S ALL YOUR FAULT, MARTHA. YOU SPOILED HIM! And so Ma Kent said,

DON'T SHIFT THE BLAME ON ME, JONATHAN KENT! HE'S YOUR SON, TOO!

And so Pa Kent picked up his suitcase and left. And Ma Kent picked up her suitcase and left. And so you felt real bad and said,

NOW I'M . . . I'M ALL ALONE . . . CHOKE!

And then you looked at their pictures and you cryed a lot and you said, OH, IF ONLY THEY WOULD COME BACK, I WOULD NEVER BE A BAD BOY AGAIN . . . SOB!

And that's when they came back.

And that's how they punished you, by making you feel bad and cry. The only trouble is that I would never feel bad if my mom and dad left me. Especially if they took Buster with them. Because then I wouldn't have to hide my comicbooks anymore. And I wouldn't have to go dump the garbage. And I wouldn't have to worry about Sister Mary Justin anymore because if she called my mom and dad they wouldn't be there.

And so this is what I'm gonna do when I get Super, Superman.

I'm gonna hide behind the statue of The Virgin Mary in

church and wait until Sister Mary Justin comes in to pray. And then I'm gonna pick it up and make it fly allover the place. And Sister Mary Justin won't know it's me and she'll think it's a miracle. And then I'll call her a SINNER! only I'll disguise my voice so it sounds like a Virgin. And then I'll say,

YOU'RE GONNA GO TO HELL, SISTER MARY JUSTIN! And she'll get real scared like I always do. And she'll say,

PLEASE, MARY . . . PLEASE DON'T SEND ME THERE . . . SOB!

And I'll fly the statue right over her head and I'll drop it right beside her and I'll make it crash into a hundred pieces and she'll put her hands over her head and start crying. And I'll say,

IT'S TOO LATE, SISTER MARY JUSTIN! HA-HA!

And the other day while we was in church I noticed that the statue wasn't wearing any shoes and it was stepping on a snake with its bare feet. Sister Mary Justin said sometimes The Devil pretends to be a snake like the time he talked to Adam and Eve. I guess it's his secret identity but I don't think it's a very good one.

So what I'm gonna do is I'm gonna get a REAL snake, Superman. And when I drop the statue then I'm gonna drop the snake too. And she'll think it came alive and The Devil's gonna get her. Only I won't make it a poisonous snake because I don't want to kill her. I just want to scare her to death.

That's why I better learn how to fly pretty soon so I can do it. So on Saturday I'm gonna climb to a higher branch of the apple tree and I'll see how far I can go and I bet it'll be REAL far, Superman. But right now I better say Goodby because Robert's done with our homework and I gotta copy it. I mean borrow it. Next time I'll do it and he'll borrow it back. My mom said you shouldn't borrow nothing unless you return it. I also have to write a letter to Jimmy Olsen for Robert so I better say goodnight. Goodnight.

Your VERYgood pals,
JERRY and ROBERT

———

DEAR JIMMY OLSEN,

This is a picture of Robert Sipanno standing in front of The Pulpburg Press with his notebook and his freckles. He don't really work for The Pulpburg Press. He just likes to stand there a lot because when he grows up he wants to be a cub reporter like certain people are. I know you can't see his freckles very good because I had to stand way across the street so we could get The Pulpburg Press sign in it. But he really does have LOTS of freckles like certain people have. And every time I read Superman comicbooks I keep calling you Jimmy Sipanno and I call him Robert Olsen and that's because you look so much alike. Except Robert's a little littler. The only trouble is that Robert is a Italien and you're not because one time Robert asked his grandma if Olsen was a Italien name and she said it sounded Polish. But except for that you're almost twins. I thought I should let you know in case you ever wanted to ask Superman to fly you to Pulpburg to meet him. So goodby.

Robert's Bestfriend,
Mr. Jerry Chariot

PS: We always read all your storys in The Daily Planet and we think you write real good scoops.

———◆———

DEAR SUPERMAN,

What you could do is you could give Mr. Mxyzptlk! a T-shirt with his name written on it frontwords like it's supposed to be. And then when he looked in the mirror his name would be spelt backwords because that's the way mirrors are. And then he would read it and he would disappear back to The Fifth Dimension with all the other imps. How do you like that one?

Your Friends,
JERRY and ROBERT

———◆———

DEAR SUPERFRIEND,

You see, what happend was Robert raised his hand. And Sister Mary Justin said YES, ROBERT, YOU MAY BE EXCUSED. And Robert said BUT I DON'T HAVE TO GO TO THE BATHROOM. And Sister Mary Justin said THEN WHY DID YOU RAISE YOUR HAND? And Robert said BECAUSE I WANT TO TELL YOU SOMETHING. And Sister Mary Justin said *YOU* WANT TO TELL *ME* SOMETHING? THIS SHOULD BE GOOD. And Robert said WELL, I THINK IT'S GOOD AND SO DOES JERRY, BUT WE DON'T KNOW IF YOU WILL. And Sister Mary Justin looked at me. And then she looked at Robert. And then she said NOW I KNOW THIS IS GOING TO BE GOOD. And Robert tryed to smile but he didn't do it too good. And then he pulled out the

World Book Encyclopedia VOL. 9 out of his desk. And all the kids started whispering. And Sister Mary Justin yelled SIT STILL! And everybody jumped except Albert Ambrozzi. And Robert dropped the book on the floor. And Jimmy Sinceri giggled. And Robert picked it up. And he brought it up to Sister Mary Justin's desk. And he set it down. And he opened it up. And Sister Mary Justin said WHAT, MAY I ASK, IS THIS? And Robert said IT'S A MAP. And Sister Mary Justin said OF COURSE IT'S A MAP, I CAN SEE THAT. And Robert said OF ILLINOISE. And Sister Mary Justin said ILLINOISE? And Robert said YES, ILLINOISE. And Janie Jobb laughed. And Sister Mary Justin looked at it. And then then she looked at me. And then Robert said SEE THIS DOT? And he pointed to it. And Sister Mary Justin bent down. And Robert looked up. And then Robert said WELL, THAT'S METROPOLIS. And here comes Robert now and he don't know I'm writing this letter and so I gotta hide it. Goodby.

JERRY

—⋅⋈⋅—

Hello, Superman,

That was close. Whew. Anyway, Sister Mary Justin's face got all red just like The Devil's. I swear. And her eyes got REAL big. And nobody in the room said anything. Not even Sister Mary Justin. She just looked at Robert and so did everybody else. And so Robert said THAT'S WHERE and he swollowed some spit THAT'S WHERE SUPERMAN LIVES. And Sister Mary Justin said SUPERMAN! And she said it so loud that even Albert jumped. And then she said SUPERMAN DOES NOT LIVE IN METROPOLIS BE-CAUSE SUPERMAN DOES NOT LIVE AT ALL! And

Robert said BUT IT'S WRITE HERE ON THE MAP. And Sister Mary Justin said THAT IS NOT WHERE SUPER-MAN LIVES! And Robert said BUT THE MAP SAYS . . . And Sister Mary Justin pounded her fist down on the map REAL hard and Robert jumped and even Jimmy Sinceri was afraid. And Sister Mary Justin said HAVE YOU EVER SEEN SUPERMAN? And Robert said No. And Sister Mary Justin said HAVE YOU EVER BEEN TO METROPOLIS? And Robert said Not yet. And Sister Mary Justin said THEN HOW DO YOU KNOW THEY EXIST? And Robert said Because I just know. And Sister Mary Justin said THAT'S IMPOSSIBLE! And Robert was gonna say some-thing but he couldn't because he was biting his nails and crying. And Sister Mary Justin grabbed his hand and said DON'T BITE YOUR NAILS! and she hit it. Hard. I could tell it hurt. And Robert looked at his red hand. And then he looked at Sister Mary Justin's red face. And then he started to yell. REALLY yell. Yell and cry at the same time. I never saw him like that before. I don't know what happend to him. But he yelled HAVE YOU EVER BEEN TO HEAVEN, HUH? HAVE YOU EVER SEEN HEAVEN? And Sister Mary Justin just looked at him. And he started to run for the door. And he was still crying. And Sister Mary Justin said COME BACK HERE YOUNG MAN! And Robert opened the door. And he turned around. And he looked Sister Mary Justin right in the eyes. And he said I BET YOU AIN'T NEVER EVEN SEEN GOD!

And he ran out.

And he ran all the way home.

And he told his mom how he never wanted to go to Holy Redeemer School again. And he was still crying. And you know what, Superman? His mom never even hit him. And neither did his dad. But they made him go back to Holy Redeemer School. But first they went in to talk to Sister

Mary Justin. And Robert's mom was REAL mad. That's why she decided to have a drink before she went in and told Sister Mary Justin that if she EVER hits their son again then they're gonna sue her and the hole convent. I mean holy convent. And so now Sister Mary Justin REALLLLLLY hates Robert only she can't hit him. And so that's even worse. And Robert's mother's name is Elizabeth. And she lets us call her Elizabeth and not Mrs. Sipanno. Except Robert. He calls her mom. And every Saturday night Elizabeth gets drunk. She used to get drunk on Friday night but then her father who was Robert's grandfather happend to die on a Friday night and so now she gets drunk on Saturday night. And last Saturday night she got REAL drunk and she said THOSE GOD DAM NUNNS! THEY CAN'T HIT MY BOY! And she grabbed Robert and she kissed him. NOT MY BOY. And you know what I wish sometimes, Superman? I wish my mom would get drunk sometimes. But she don't.

Goodby.

Just,
Jerry

PS: Robert don't know I wrote you this letter because then he'd feel REAL bad and he wouldn't talk to me ever again. But I figure if he don't know I wrote it then he can't feel bad. And since you never write back anyway, I don't have to worry about it. So if you ever decide to write us a letter, please don't mention it. Thanks, Man of Steel.

———⊶⊰⊷———

DEAR SUPERMAN,
You see, my mom's got this towel which is REAL old

and it's got a hole in it and so I figured she won't miss it. And what I did was I got a Magic Marker and I put a S on the back of it and that stands for Super Jerry. I wanted to put SJ on it but then Robert said that might stand for Sister Mary Justin and so we just put a S on it like yours. I hope you don't mind. And I usually climb to the second branch but this time I climbed to the third. And I put my hands out in front of me. And Robert said ARE YOU READY?

And I said YES.

And Robert said I'LL COUNT TO THREE OK?

And he did.

And I flew REAL good, Superman. Only I didn't land too good and that's why my foot still hurts. Only I can't tell my mom because she'll get mad because I wasn't supposed to be up that high. Especially with a cape on. So Robert said maybe I should become indestructable before I learn how to fly and this way I won't get hurt just in case I don't do it. But you just wait, Superman. I'll do it. You'll see. I KNOW I'll do it because I REALLY want to, Superman. You'll see.

GETTING SUPER,

JERRY

———

Dear SUPERMAN,

The other day my brother Buster asked me who I liked better than anybody else in the hole world. The reason he asked me was because he wanted me to ask him the same question back. Because Buster is a lot older than me and so he likes girls and he likes this one girl named Mary Louise quite a bit. So he wanted to tell me how he likes her more than ANYBODY in the hole world even though she's got a bigger nose than he's got. And so I said SUPERMAN. And he said WHAT? And I said I LIKE SUPERMAN BETTER THAN ANYBODY ELSE IN THE HOLE WORLD. And he said YOU MUST BE A QUEER. And I said WHAT'S A QUEER? And he said BOYS ARE SUPPOSED TO LIKE GIRLS NOT BOYS. LIKE ME. I LIKE MARY LOUISE. BOY DO I LIKE MARY LOUISE. MAYBE I EVEN LOVE HER. And I said WHAT'S A QUEER? again. And he said THAT'S A BOY WHO LIKES OTHER BOYS. THAT'S A SISSIE. And I said I AIN'T NO SISSIE! And he said YES YOU ARE IF YOU LIKE SUPERMAN. And I said NO I AIN'T! And he said SISSIEEEEEEEEEE! And I said WELL I THINK SUPER-MAN IS BETTER THAN MARY LOUISE ANY DAY. SHE'S GOT A BIG NOSE AND SHE'S ALWAYS GOT PIMPELS ON HER CHIN. And Buster said DON'T SAY THAT ABOUT MARY LOUISE! I LOVE HER! And I said WELL IT'S TRUE. And he got real mad and hit me real hard. And then he called me a queer again. And then he said Superman's probly a queer too. And then he walked away.

And so me and Robert talked about it quite a bit and then we decided to ask Robert's bigbrother Bruno what a queer was and Bruno said it was something REAL bad and we couldn't find out about it until after we got older. And Robert said WHY? And Bruno said BECAUSE IT'S A SIN and so he couldn't even talk about it. And Sister Mary Justin never told us about that sin before so maybe we should ask her about it. Except Robert won't do it and I don't think I will either. But we figure if it's REAL bad then you can't be one. Not you, Superman. You're perfect. And since you're perfect, you must know what a queer is. So what is it please? Thank you very much.

YOUR FRIENDS,
JERRY and ROBERT

DEAR SUPERMAN,

The other day in Religion class Sister Mary Justin told us a story about a little kid who was gonna make his First Holy Communion. So first he had to make his First Holy Confession so he could tell the priest all his sins and be forgiven. Which he did. Except he forgot one of them on purpose because it was a MORTAL SIN and he was afraid.

And when it came time to make his First Holy Communion and he was all dressed up in his brand new First Holy Communion suit and he was on his way to the church with his mom and dad and everybody else in his entire family, that's when he started thinking about that Mortal Sin which was crawling around inside of him like a snake.

And then it came time to make his First Holy Communion and EVERY seat in the church was filled and some people were even standing and he walked up to the alter and he knelt down and he closed his eyes and everybody watched as he stuck out his tongue like you're supposed to do when the priest is gonna give it to you. And then the priest gave it to him. And then you know what happend, Superman?

He felt something real hot in his mouth. So he opened his eyes and there was blood dripping allover his chin and his neck and his brand new First Holy Communion suit. It was the blood of The Baby Jesus and it meant he was gonna go to HELL for sure. That's what Sister Mary Justin said. She said our sins drive NAILS into The Baby Jesus if we don't confess them. She looked right at me when she said that.

That's why I GOTTA find out if I'm a queer, Superman. Because if I am and if it's a Mortal Sin, then what's gonna happen when me and Robert make our First Holy Communion? Because I figure if I'm a queer then Robert's probly one too. Goodby.

> Your Friends,
> JERRY CHARIOT and ROBERT

You see, Superman,

Sister Mary Justin said one Mortal Sin is worse than a HUNDRED venial sins because a venial sin is just a little one like telling a lie or not doing your own homework. But a Mortal Sin is a BIG one like murdering somebody or not going to Mass on Sunday. And Robert said CAN WE GO TO ANOTHER CHURCH INSTEAD OF MASS? And Sister Mary Justin said NO, YOU HAVE TO GO TO MASS OR ELSE IT'S A MORTAL SIN! So that means all the Protestents and Negros and everybody else is going to Hell. And so are the queers maybe. Except we're not too sure. But Robert said we better make sure Superman's a Catholic just in case he runs into a piece of Kryptonite and goes to Hell. It'd be really AWFUL if we ended up in Heaven or someplace else without you, Superman. That's why I'm sending you my Catechism because it explains EVERYTHING you need to know about to become a real Catholic just in case you're not already. So if you are, please pass it on to Supergirl if she needs it. Or else you could give it to Jimmy Olsen. But we don't think you should give it to Lois Lane even if she's a Protestent.

> Your Pals,
> Jerry AND Robert

Dear Superman,

Me and Robert can't stop thinking about it and we decided that it don't matter if you go to Hell or not because the flames can't hurt you anyway because you're indestructable even after you die. And then if you wanted, you could fly to Heaven and visit me and Robert and Jimmy Olsen for a while. And since everybody in Heaven would already be happy and have wings and everything then they wouldn't need you anyway. So you could go back to Hell and use your Super-breath to cool off all those people down there because they sure could use it. That's what Robert Sipanno said. He said God probly doesn't even want you to become a Catholic. He probly WANTS you to go to Hell and save people after you die. So why don't you give my Catechism to Jimmy Olsen and tell him Robert said HI. Goodby.

JERRY CHARIOT and ROBERT SIPANNO

PS: Besides, if you went to Hell then Mr. Mxyzptlk! would never go there to bother you because NOBODY wants to go to Hell. Not even a imp.

DEAR SUPERMAN,

The other day my mom caught Buster doing something he wasn't supposed to be doing with his Thing. He was in the bedroom doing it when my mom walked in and he didn't know it until she started yelling. BOY did she yell! I don't know exactly what Buster was doing but I heard my mom and dad whispering about it later. My mom told my dad how Buster was looking at a picture of Mary Louise Wesson while he was doing it. And then she started crying. And my dad said ALL KIDS DO IT AT PUBERTY. And I don't know what puberty is but it must be something in the bedroom because that's where he was doing it at. And so my mom said IT'S NOT NORMEL! And when I heard that I figured maybe it was a good chance to find out what a queer was. So I said MAYBE IT'S QUEER and my mom and dad looked up. I guess they didn't know I was listening. But BOY did they get mad, Superman! Especially my mom. She didn't even wait for my dad to get up and hit me. She did it herself. Then she said I was a ROTTEN LITTLE BRAT and she smacked me right across the face. Real hard. Then she told me to get out of her site, RIGHT THIS INSTANT, DO YOU HEAR ME YOUNG MAN? So I went to look for Buster because I figured since we're BOTH in trouble then maybe he'd like me a little more now. But he didn't because when I asked him what he was doing with his Thing he said GET LOST! And then he hit me across the face like my mom did. And that's why I don't like groan ups, Superman. Except Mrs. Bacchio. Because groan ups always yell at you and hit you and tell you what you have to do all the time. And you can't do nothing about it. Not until you get big enough to hit somebody like Buster hits me sometimes. Because then you're not so little anymore because somebody else is littler because everybody wants to be bigger than somebody, Superman. But not me. I want to be bigger than EVERYBODY. I want to be

> Your friend,
> SUPER-JERRY

PS: And someday I will.

DEAR SUPERMAN,

Just in case you don't know what a Thing is that's the Thing you pee out of. Except you don't have to pee because you're Super. But I do. And so that's what a Thing is. And I wonder if that's what Buster was doing, peeing in the bedroom? I wouldn't like it either if I was my mom. But I'm not. I'm just me. So what do you think?

Your Pal Jerry Again

PS: Since you don't have to pee because you're Super then maybe you don't have a Thing. But if you didn't have a Thing then you'd be a girl. But you're not a girl. You're Superman. And if you don't pee out of it, then what do you do with it? Robert said maybe it has a special power like your eyes have X-ray Vision. Is that it?

━━━━⊰⊱━━━━

Dear SUPERPAL,

The other day guess what? Well, Sister Mary Justin noticed I didn't have my Catechism and so she asked me where it was? And I said I gave it to a friend so he wouldn't go to Hell. And she said YOU WHAT? And I said he wasn't a Catholic and he wanted to become one and so I gave it to him. And you know what, Superman? She thought that was real nice. She really did. She even smiled at me which she never did before. And then she asked me who I gave it to? And I said it's a secret. And she said maybe she could go talk to him and help him become a Catholic so who is it? And I said I better not tell you. And she stopped smiling and she said I might go to Hell because maybe she might be able to save him and I'll stop her SO TELL ME, JEROME! So I knew it'd be just as bad if I didn't tell her as if I did tell her. So I told her. And that's why the rest of this story is just like the other ones only I didn't cry, Superman. So maybe I'm getting used to it. Or else maybe I'm getting Super like you. I sure hope so.

YOUR FRIEND JERRY
and Robert

PS: We've been looking pretty close at the comicbooks and we even got a magnifying glass that Robert's brother Bruno uses for his coin collection. And it don't look like your Thing is very Super but I can't really tell since you always wear a swimming suit over your leotards. And so is it? I told Robert it MUST be but we're not very sure.

———✂———

Dear Man of Steel,

Yesterday in Religion class Sister Mary Justin said men are better than women because Eve listened to The Devil first when he pretended to be a snake. And then Adam listened to Eve. And so they both got in trouble. And that's why women aren't good enough to be priests and so they have to be nunns. And that's why girls can't be alterboys. And that's why God had a son and not a daughter. And that's why God the Father isn't God the Mother. And I don't know what the Holy Ghost is because Sister Mary Justin said he's a bird and not a person. But you know what I'm beginning to think, Superman?

I'm beginning to think that Things must be more importent than anything else. Even souls. Because women are allowed to have souls too. I think. And you know what else I think? I think the BIGGER your Thing is then the stronger you are. I mean, look at women—they don't have anyThing and that's why they're so weak. And look at my dad. His Thing is a LOT bigger than Buster's and that's why he's stronger. And Buster's Thing is bigger than mine and that's why he's stronger. And so your Thing must be the BIGGEST Thing in the world, Superman, because you're stronger than ANYBODY.

That's why we're sending you Robert's ruler. I already sent you my Catechism and so now it's Robert's turn to send you something. What we want you to do is measure it and then tell us how long it is. And if one ruler isn't enough then you'll have to buy another one. Or maybe you could get a yard stick. Anyway, if you tell me how long it is then I'll know how long I have to wait until I become SUPER like you. I hope it won't be very long. Goodby.

Your BESTfriends,
JERRY CHARIOT and ROBERT

PS: I measured mine last night and it's a inch and another little line. That's pretty good isn't it?

⎯⎯⎯✂⎯⎯⎯

DEAR SUPERMAN,

The other day on Monday I asked Mrs. Bacchio if she thought Superman was a Catholic and she thought about it for a while. And then she smiled. And then she said I NEVER REALLY THOUGHT ABOUT IT BEFORE, BUT I GUESS IT'S POSSIBLE.

And I said WELL WOULD YOU WANT HIM TO BE A CATHOLIC OR WOULDN'T YOU?

And she said I THINK THAT WOULD BE NICE.

And I said SO DO I AND SO DOES ROBERT.

And Robert said AND SO DOES GOD.

And she laughed and said YES, HE PROBABLY DOES.

And so I don't care what the other kids say because I'm GLAD I sent you my Catechism, Superman. And I think it's too bad that Mrs. Bacchio is a woman because I really like her a LOT. And so does Robert Sipanno. And we think God should of created Mrs. Bacchio instead of Eve because then Adam probly wouldn't of got in all that trouble. But I guess Adam and Mrs. Bacchio wouldn't sound as good as Adam and Eve. And besides, if Mrs. Bacchio was Eve then Eve would probly be Mrs. Bacchio and then we'd NEVER get any free comicbooks.

So maybe it's better this way after all.

YOUR PALS,
JERRY and ROBERT

PS: Me and Robert just figured out a REALLY good way to trick Mr. Mxyzptlk! What you could do is ask him to be on the Mickey Mouse Club show because he's a imp and so he already looks like a Mousekateer anyway. And besides it's one of my FAVORITEST programs and I NEVER miss it and I just KNOW all the Mickey Mousekateers would help you get rid of him. And the way you could do it is wait until the end of the show when Karen and Cubby and Annette and Jimmy and everybody sings M-I-CCCCCCC . . . K-E-YYYYYYY . . . M-O-U-S-EEEEEEE . . . Only you could change it to !-K-LLLLLLL . . . L-T-PPPPPPP . . . P-Z-Y-X-MMMMMMM . . . and then he would disappear in front of me and Annette and Robert and everybody else who was watching. Isn't that a GOOD one?

Dear Jimmy Olsen,

Robert just read that story about you and that UGLY monster and so did I and we both HATED it. It was really terrible how he came from that other planet and he wouldn't let you alone and he followed you everywhere and he scared everybody because he was so ugly. Even uglier than Mary Louise Wesson. And so nobody wanted to be your friend anymore because that monster followed you everywhere and he even slept with you. And you tried to get rid of him but you couldn't because Superman wasn't around to help you. He was out in outer space for a while. So finally the monster said he would leave you alone if you went back to his world with him for just two hours. And you HAD to get rid of him and so you said OK. Only when you got back to his world you started scaring everybody because they thought YOU was ugly. When actually all of THEM was ugly. And so you felt real bad. And so Robert wanted me to write you this letter and tell you how he thinks you're pretty handsome. And so does everybody else except Sister Mary Justin. And we know what it's like when nobody likes you very much and everybody calls you names. Especially Jimmy Sinceri. So we want you to know that we like you ALL the time. And we'll ALWAYS be your friends even if you really do get ugly. And if you ever decide to become a Catholic then FOR SURE we will. So don't worry.

Your PALS,
ROBERT SIPANNO and JERRY CHARIOT

DEAR SUPERMAN,

I know this might sound really dumb but my mom just said she's gonna give me a baby brother for Christmas. And I said ARE YOU SURE?

And she said YES, I'M POSITIVE.

And I said WELL WHAT IF I DON'T WANT ONE?

And she said WHAT DO YOU MEAN?

And I said WELL WHAT IF I WANT SOMETHING ELSE?

And she said LIKE WHAT?

And I said LIKE A CAPTAIN NEMO ATOMIC SUBMARINE DO-IT-YOURSELF ASSEMBLY KIT WHICH COSTS ONLY $9 and 95¢. PLUS TACKS. WHICH IS PROBLY A LOT CHEAPER THAN A BABY BROTHER ANYWAY.

And she just looked at me and smiled. And then she said it might be a sister but it'll probly be a brother because that's what she wants.

And I said THAT'S NOT WHAT I WANT.

And she said GO DUMP THE GARBAGE. That's what she always says when she don't want to say anything else.

And I know that Christmas is a loooong time away yet and so maybe she'll change her mind. But I don't think she will because she looked like she really meant it. I could tell. And besides, I don't really want a baby brother because then he wouldn't like me just like I don't like Buster. I'd rather be a little brother than a big brother because they're not as mean.

That's why I was wondering where my baby brother is right now, Superman? I mean, where do you go before you're borned and you're nothing? I know it's not Heaven or Hell so maybe it's Purgatory. Or is there another place we don't know about yet? And do you think I could pray to him wherever he is? And then I could ask him to PLEASE not be borned until after Christmas and then I could get that submarine I was telling you about.

What do you think?

> Your friend,
> JERRY CHARIOT

——◆——

DEAR SUPERMAN,

You see, Robert's mother Elizabeth used to be really fat. Even fatter than she usually is. And she's usually really fat. That's because she's a Italien like Robert is. But one time she was fatter than she's ever been before and she kept on getting fatter. And then she had another Italien baby which turned out to be Sue Ann. And I thought it was because she kept eating all the time and that's why she was getting extra fat. And one night she even got up at 4 o'clock in the morning and she ate all of Robert's fudgsickels and Robert was really mad. And so was I because he gives some of them to me sometimes. And so this is what Robert thinks. Robert thinks it wasn't really fat but it was Sue Ann because Sue Ann really loves fudgsickels. But Robert's mom don't. And so she was eating them for Sue Ann who was really the fat because it wasn't fat. Because everybody knows that babys love fudgsickels. And so do me and Robert. Except we're not babys. We just happen to love them. So what do you think, Superman? Is my baby brother really in my mom's stomick like Sue Ann Sipanno? We'd sure like to know.

> YOUR FRIENDS,
> JERRY and ROBERT

Dear SuperPAL,

The other day Sister Mary Justin said we're all children of God even people who aren't children. Like my mom and Elizabeth and Old Lady Holbrook. She said that's because God made everybody in the hole world especially Catholics. And I said EVEN BABY BROTHERS?

And she said SIT DOWN, JEROME! And then she said YES, EVEN BABY BROTHERS AND SISTERS AND EVERYBODY.

And I said HOW DOES HE DO IT?

And she said WHAT?

And I said HOW DOES GOD MAKE BABYS BECAUSE I THOUGHT MOTHERS DID THAT?

And she said WHO TOLD YOU THAT?

And I said ROBERT SIPANNO.

And she said ROBERT, STAND UP!

So Robert stood up.

So then she said YOU BOYS WILL REMAIN AFTER SCHOOL. WE WILL TALK ABOUT THIS LATER!

And Robert said WHY? WE JUST ASKED YOU A QUESTION? And she looked at Robert real mean and I could tell she was wishing she could hit him. And Robert said ALL WE WANT TO KNOW IS WHAT GOD MAKES BABYS OUT OF?

And Sister Mary Justin said GOD MAKES BABYS OUT OF LOVE, ROBERT. THAT IS ALL YOU NEED TO KNOW. NOW NO MORE OF YOUR DIRTY QUESTIONS!

And I said IS LOVE DIRTY?

And she said OF COURSE NOT.

And Robert said WHERE DOES HE GET ALL THAT LOVE FROM?

74

And Sister Mary Justin said GOD IS LOVE.

And I said I THOUGHT HE WAS JESUS.

And Sister Mary Justin said BE QUIET!! And then she turned real red and she said YOU WILL REPORT TO THE PRINCIPLE'S OFFICE! I WILL DEAL WITH YOU LATER!

And then it was later and she came to deal with us. And she said we were the worst students she EVER had and we were even worser than when she had Negros in Erie. And we're always making trouble and she's getting sick and tired of it. And if it happens JUST ONE MORE TIME then she's gonna expell us from school and we won't be able to make our First Holy Communion and we'll have to go to the public school and become Protestents and go to Hell.

And you know what, Superman? She never said if it's God or my mom who's gonna make my baby brother.

JERRY and ROBERT again

———✦———

DEAR SUPERMAN,

Me and Robert just read the story where Jimmy Olsen told you to DROP DEAD! And then he told you to BEAT IT! And then he told you to GET LOST, SUPER-CHUMP! And you thought he hated you and so did everybody else in Metropolis, Illinoise. Including Jimmy. Only it turned out it was that SPACE JEWEL that made him feel the opposit of how he REALLY feels. Because if he really hated you then he would have loved you. So I'm glad you figured it out on the last page like you always do. And then it showed you and Jimmy flying through the air and you were both smiling and you had your arm around Jimmy's shoulder and I got little pimpels allover me and Robert. We both

75

wished we was Jimmy so we could go for a ride with you. We'd really like that a HOLE LOT. Especially me.

And so someday when I get Super then I'm gonna take Robert on a ride JUST like that. After I learn how to fly pretty soon. And when I fly him to Holy Redeemer School then he can wave at all the kids who are looking up and pointing at us. And then I'll fly him through the window and right into his seat in front of Sister Mary Justin. And then I'll fly out again. And then I'll sneak into the lavatory and change into my regular clothes so nobody will know that Jerry Chariot is my secret identity. And then I'll walk up the steps and Janie Jobb will be standing there waiting for me. And she'll say, "Where were you when Superkid went flying by?" And I'll say, "I was in the lavatory going to the bathroom." And she'll say, "Hmmmmmmmmmmm." And then she'll say, "Isn't it funny that I never see you and Superkid around at the same time?" And I'll say, "That sure is funny, Janie. Ha-ha!" And then I'll walk away. And then on the next page I'll be back in the classroom and everybody will be in their seats and Janie Jobb will be thinking, "Gee, I wonder if he really is Superkid?" And then it will say THE END.

YOUR FRIEND,
JERRY CHARIOT

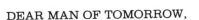

DEAR MAN OF TOMORROW,

How are you today? We are fine thanks. We just read that story called THE RADIOACTIVE BOY which was in GIANT SUPERMAN'S PAL JIMMY OLSEN NO. 13. Which was right after the story about how Jimmy didn't really hate you. Which is what I wrote about yesterday. Which is why I'm writing again, Superman. You see, I thought Jimmy was gonna die FOR SURE when he got exposed to that radioactive stuff. That's why he ran out in the woods because his body was glowing allover and he was thinking,

"Scientists say anybody getting an overdose of atomic radiations could only live . . . (Gasp!) . . . a few hours!"

And that's when he noticed a cave and so he ran inside and it was REAL dark but he was still glowing and thinking, "Yet I—I can't call anybody here to spend my last moments with me . . . He would die, too!"

And then Jimmy started to cry and then Robert started to cry and then I started to cry because EVERYBODY thought Jimmy was gonna die. Even you, Superman. That's why you went out looking for him with your X-ray Vision until finally you found that cave and flew inside and said, "It's I, Jimmy—Superman! I found you!"

And Jimmy said, "Your voice sounds so sad . . . You must know the truth about me, Superman!"

And you said, "Yes! Poor Jimmy . . . (Choke!)"

And then you turned around and sat down on a rock and said, "But—but for once I'm unable to save you, Jimmy! Oh, Jimmy . . . My poor pal . . ."

And we NEVER saw you cry like that before, Superman. That's why we was crying with you. Because it was really AWFUL. We didn't know what to do. We just kept crying and reading and getting page 33 all wet. And also 34. And then Robert's mom heard us and so she came in and wanted to know WHAT'S WRONG? And Robert tried to tell her except he was crying too much. So I told her. And you know what, Superman? She didn't even yell or nothing. My mom probly would of hit us. But Robert's mom just looked at us and then she touched Robert on the shoulder and said,

"My, my . . ."

And then she smiled and said, "Well, if it's that important then you should cry . . ."

And then she kissed Robert on the cheek. And then she kissed me on the hair. And then she walked out . . .

And then we turned the page and found out Jimmy wasn't gonna die after all. And BOY were we glad! Especially Robert. Because we know we hardly ever get letters from you, Superman, but we still like you and Jimmy Olsen better than ANYBODY else we know. Even God or Mrs. Bacchio or ourselfs. And we like them quite a bit. And so we don't even care if we NEVER get to meet you or go for a ride with you or anything, as long as you stay alive and make sure that Jimmy does also. Of course we still want to meet you an awful lot, Superman. But if we can't, then we'd rather not meet you because you're alive than because you're dead. So PLEASE be extra careful please.

Thank you very VERY much.

LOVE,
Jerry and Robert

———◆———

Well, Superman,

Me and Robert have been thinking about it a loooooooooong time and we finally found a REALLY good way to get Mr. Mxyzptlk! to say his name backwords and disappear. What you could do is you could ask him to play a game called FAMOUS NAMES because he really likes

78

games because he's a imp and not a person. And that's what me and Robert like to play sometimes. Like I might say WHAT IS THE NAME OF SUPERMAN'S FAMOUS DOG?

And Robert would say KRYPTO.

Or I might say WHAT IS THE NAME OF GOD'S FAMOUS SON?

And Robert would say THE BABY JESUS.

And so you could say WHAT IS THE NAME THAT THE FAMOUS IMP SAYS BACKWORDS?

And he would say !KLTPZYXM and then he would disappear. If he was dumb. Which he isn't. So he'll say,

HA-HA, YOU'RE TRYING TO TRICK ME, SUPERMAN!

And you'll say, WELL, I GUESS IT ISN'T VERY FAMOUS ANYWAY.

And he'll say YES IT IS!

And you'll say NO IT ISN'T.

And he'll say YES IT IS! again.

And you'll say WHAT IS?

And he'll say !KLTPZYXM. Except he might be smarter than you think, Superman. And he'll say,

I WON'T SAY IT, SUPERMAN!

And you'll say THAT'S BECAUSE YOU DON'T KNOW IT, MR. MXYZPTLK!

And he'll say YES I DO!

And you'll say YOU SURE ARE A DUMB IMP!

And he'll say NO I'M NOT!

And you'll say DON'T EVEN KNOW YOUR OWN NAME BACKWORDS—HA-HA!

And he'll say YES I DO!

And you'll say THEN WHAT IS IT?

And he'll say !KLTPZYXM and then FOR SURE he'll disappear. And we know all that talking is gonna take up a lot of space in the comicbook but we hope you can do it anyway. So GOOD LUCK, Man of Steel!

Your VERYgood PALS,
JERRY and ROBERT

PS: We hope you'll write and tell us if you like it for a change.

The
Third
Dimension

DEAR SUPERMAN,

Right now Robert and me are on the Duck Rock but what I wanted to tell you about happend this morning when Veronica who lives nextdoor went to talk to Old Lady Holbrook. Except she don't really talk because she whispers like she always does. Like one time she kept whispering about Robert's mom and how she gets drunk all the time because she must be a alkaholic. And another time she kept whispering about somebody who was a mother who had a baby who didn't have a father and Old Lady Holbrook whisperd I CAN'T BELIEVE IT!

And Veronica nextdoor whisperd I'M TELLING YOU, MARGRET, I GOT IT STRAIGHT FROM THE HORSE'S NEIGHBOR.

And this morning Veronica was walking up the street REAL fast and she didn't even knock because Old Lady Holbrook was waiting for her on the porch. So we figured they had something real importent to whisper about and it would take a LONG time. That's why I waited for them to go inside before I snuck out of the bushes and put on my cape and climbed up the tree and Robert said READY?

And I said READY.

Only I guess I wasn't because my cape got caught on a branch and I almost got hung like a cowboy. Except the knot broke as Veronica opened the door and came out and went right over to see my mom. So I figured I was really gonna get it.

That's why I sneaked home and took off my shoes and tip-toed in the doorway and you know what, Superman?

She wasn't even saying nothing about it for a change. That's because she was too busy whispering about how Mrs. Bacchio was doing something with somebody who she wasn't supposed to be doing it with. And I don't know exactly what it was because I never heard them whisper THAT low before. But it must of been pretty bad because my mom said HOW DISGUSTING!

And Veronica said I'M TELLING YOU, FRANCES, THAT LENORE BACCHIO IS A DEMON!

And that's why I don't like Veronica very much because she whispers like that about EVERYBODY. And so does my mom. And so the next time they whisper about Mrs. Bacchio I'll let you know what she wasn't supposed to be doing with whoever she was doing it with. If I figure it out.

So long, Superman.

Your pals,
JERRY and ROBERT

Well, Superman,

Whatever Mrs. Bacchio did she must still be doing it because my mom and Veronica nextdoor have been whispering about it for three days. And I don't know what it is but I know she was doing it with a man and it wasn't Mr. Bacchio. That's because my mom whisperd DOES HER HUSBAND KNOW ABOUT IT?

And Veronica whisperd NO, BUT EVERYBODY ELSE DOES.

And I said I DON'T.

And my mom looked up. And so did Veronica. And

they thought I was watching Mickey Mouse Club only I wasn't. I was listening to them. And so I said WHO IS SHE DOING IT WITH?

And boy did my mom get mad! She yelled at me and told me how I wasn't supposed to listen to groan ups talk. Especially when they're whispering. And how I better get outside before she gives me a beating. So I went up to Robert's house and we talked about it for a long time and we tried to figure out who it was she's doing it with. Whatever it is she's doing. And Robert said it must be somebody REALLY bad for them to whisper so much. And so I said maybe it's you, Superman, because why else would my mom get so mad? So if it is you, then why don't you write us a letter and tell us? And if it's not you, then don't worry about writing.

Except you probly wouldn't write even if it was you. So maybe you better write even if it's not you.

Thank you, Superpal.

> JERRY CHARIOT
> and
> ROBERT SIPANNO

DEAR SUPERMAN,

Well, we know who she's doing it with and it's not you. It's Mr. Durrelli. He's the one who brings the comicbooks after school every Monday when me and Robert wait. And so now you don't have to write us that letter and tell us who it is. But you could tell us what it is. If you want. We haven't figured that out yet. But we figured out where it is. It's in the back of Mrs. Bacchio's News Stand where she keeps all the old comicbooks and stuff. That's what Robert's mom said when she was talking to Olivia Mariotti on the phone. Except Robert calls her Ant Olivia. And Robert's mom said that my mom said that Veronica nextdoor said that she was doing it right there in the back of the store and CAN YOU BELIEVE IT?

And then Olivia said something and Robert's mom said WHY IT'S JUST TERRIBLE! HOW MANY KIDS DOES HE HAVE?

And Olivia said something else and Robert's mom said SIX! And then she said, THAT GOES TO SHOW YOU, OLIVIA, YOU JUST CAN'T TRUST A MAN!

And so if she don't trust a man then she probly don't trust a boy either. So we better not ask her what Mrs. Bacchio was doing. But we thought maybe you could tell us since you have Super branes and also X-ray Vision. All you have to do is fly over Bacchio's News Stand and look through the roof and watch them doing it. Whatever they're doing. And then you could fly up to the Duck Rock and tell me and Robert about it. We sure would appreciate it, Man of Steel.

YOUR FRIEND JERRY and ROBERT again

PS: I like Mrs. Bacchio a LOT better than Veronica next-door or Olivia Mariotti or even my mom or Robert's mom. Or Buster or Sister Mary Justin or Jimmy Sinceri. Or my sister the Sister who is becoming a nunn who we're going to see next Sunday. Or ANYBODY. And so I don't care what they say, Superman, because I know she couldn't do nothing bad. Because I just KNOW it. So goodby.

Dear SUPERMAN,

You know what I think? I think my baby brother REALLY is in my mom's stomick. Because the other day she was holding her stomick and telling me how she's gonna call him Christopher after he's borned. And I said CHRISTOPHER?

And she said YES, ISN'T THAT NICE?

And I said HOW DO YOU SPELL THAT?

And so she wrote it down for me like this:

C H R I S T O P H E R

And I said CAN WE CALL HIM CHRIST FOR SHORT?

And she said NO, THAT'D BE A SIN.

And I said WHY?

And she said BECAUSE THERE'S ONLY ONE CHRIST AND YOU CAN'T NAME A PERSON AFTER A GOD.

And I said WHY? again.

And she said BECAUSE PEOPLE ARE JUST PEOPLE AND GOD IS GOD AND SO GOD WOULDN'T LIKE IT.

And I said WELL, I DON'T THINK WE SHOULD CALL HIM CHRISTOPHER.

And so she got to say WHY? this time.

And I said BECAUSE IT'S TOO LONG AND BESIDES IT'S UGLY.

And she said we could call him CHRIS if we want.

And I said I DON'T LIKE THAT EITHER.

And she said WELL, WHAT DO YOU LIKE?

And I said HOW ABOUT CLARK?

And she said CLARK?

And I said I THINK CLARK IS A REAL NICE NAME FOR A BABY. OR EVEN A PERSON.

And she said CLARK? again.

AND BESIDES, HE'S *MY* BABY BROTHER AND IF I

CAN'T GET A ATOMIC SUBMARINE THEN I SHOULD GET TO CALL HIM CLARK. SO THAT'S WHAT I'M GONNA DO.

So she said WE'LL TALK ABOUT IT LATER.

So I said WE TALK ABOUT EVERYTHING LATER.

So she said DON'T GET SMART WITH ME, YOUNG MAN! GO DUMP THE GARBAGE.

So I started to say something back but then my dad came in from work and so I didn't because he gets mad quicker than my mom does. And after I dumped the garbage I thought about it for quite a bit. And I decided if I can't call him Clark then maybe I could call him KAL-EL. That's what your name used to be when you lived on Krypton before it exploded. But I still like CLARK the best.

Goodby.

YOUR FRIEND JERRY

PS: Which one do you like the best?

Guess what, Superman?

My mom said we can't name my baby brother Kal-El either because all Catholic babys have to be named after Saints. And that's why we can't call him Clark. And Christ wasn't a Saint because he was God. It would be a sin if we named him after God or a person and that's why we have to name him after a Saint like Christopher even if we don't like it.

Which I don't.

You see, Superman, a Saint is somebody who used to be a person before he became a Saint. And if you want to become a Saint then somebody has to kill you first because you believe in God and they don't. Like Joan of Ark who's on a lot of the Holy Cards. She kept smiling and praying and singing about God while they tied her up and burnt her. The only trouble is that everybody here in Pulpburg already believes in God. So the only way they might kill you around here is if you DIDN'T believe in God. But I don't think that counts. So I guess I can never become a Saint. And I guess I can never name him CLARK either.

I'm sorry, Superman. I tried.

JERRY CHARIOT

PS: I don't want to be a Saint anyway because there's already a Saint named Saint Jerome. I'd hate to go to all the trouble of becoming a Saint and then have everybody get me mixed up with somebody else when they're praying to me.

———

Dear Superman,

This afternoon me and Robert went into Bacchio's News Stand to buy SUPERMAN'S PAL JIMMY OLSEN NO. 125 like we always do. That's the one where Jimmy Olsen is making you cry allover the cover so he could get some Super tears for his magic formula that he was making. So first we looked through it like we always do. That's so we can give Mrs. Bacchio some time to decide if maybe she wants to give it to us free. But she wasn't even looking at us. And she didn't smile or say HI BOYS like she always usually does sometimes. So we went over to pay for it and that's when we noticed her eyes were all red and watery like yours on the cover. And like Elizabeth's on Saturday night. And she looked really TERRIBLE, Superman. So Robert said HI, MRS. BACCHIO! and I said YOU SURE LOOK NICE TODAY but she didn't say nothing. Not even one word like Hello. She just took our money and gave us our change and didn't even look in our eyes.

And we never saw her like that before and that's why you GOTTA do something, Superman.

You see, Mrs. Bacchio really likes you a hole lot like we do. And she ALWAYS talks about you. And so we know you could make her feel better because she really feels bad because we can tell. We just know. And we don't know why exactly, but we know you could figure it out please? All you gotta do is go talk to her for a little while and she'd REALLY like that. And if you did, then me and Robert wouldn't even care if you didn't get a chance to talk to Perry White about giving Robert a job. Which is what we was gonna ask you about. But now you don't have to worry about it. Unless you wanted to. Goodby.

Love,
Jerry and Robert

PS: Did you ever hear of Saint Buster? Well I didn't either. But my mom said that Buster isn't his real name because it's Anthony like my dad. And Anthony is a real good Italien Saint. And I said ARE YOU SURE THERE ISN'T A SAINT CLARK? And she said DID YOU EVER HEAR OF HIM? And I said WELL I DON'T KNOW TOO MUCH ABOUT SAINTS, BUT SISTER MARY JUSTIN DOES. So me and Robert are gonna ask her. But first we thought you might know since your name is Clark sometimes. So if you don't know, then maybe you could fly faster than the speed of light and crash through the Time Barrier and fly back to when you was Superbaby in Smallville. And you could ask Ma and Pa Kent if they named you after Saint Clark. And then you could fly back to the future. Which is the present. Which is when me and Robert is writing this letter. Which is the way you could let us know. Thanks, Man of Steel.

Dear Clark,

We keep reading how you fly back through the TIME BARRIER a lot. Like the time you went back so you could use your Super-breath to help Benjamin Franklin fly a kite. And another time you flew back to when there was dinasores allover the Earth which was a LONG time ago. In fact it was so long ago that we can't even remember which issue it was in.

And so if you decided to fly back to see Ma and Pa Kent, then you'd also see yourself wouldn't you? I mean, you might run into yourself when you was SUPERBOY or SUPERBABY or even before you wasn't anything, like my baby brother.

And then you could watch yourself and see what you did when you was a kid.

Unless you landed in the past on a day when Superboy was in the future seeing what he was gonna look like when he became Superman. And then neither of you would get to see yourself. Unless you passed yourself on your way through the Time Barrier.

Me and Robert was wondering if that ever happend? Or if it's ever gonna happen? Why don't you tell us?

Your Friends,
JERRY CHARIOT and Robert

PS: That's why I can't wait until I get Super, Superman. Because then I can fly back through the Time Barrier and meet me when I was a kid. Which is RIGHT NOW. Which means I might be meeting myself any day now. Then I'll know what I'm gonna look like when I get Super. So I hope I come to visit me REAL soon. Goodby.

Well, SUPERMAN,

Me and Robert have been watching pretty close, but we don't see anybody who looks like me flying around. In fact we don't see anybody flying around at all. Not even you.

I hope that don't mean I'm not gonna get SUPER.

Maybe it just means that when I get Super I'm never gonna decide to fly through the Time Barrier. Except that's one of the FIRST things I'm gonna do.

So maybe it just means I'm gonna fly into a Saturday because we don't have school on Saturday and so I'll have more fun with myself. And since tomorrow is Saturday, maybe that's when I'm gonna do it.

I'll let you know.

Your,
PAL JERRY

Dear Superman,

Well I didn't do it. I didn't fly into the past and meet myself or anything. I even went up to the Duck Rock and looked allover the place and Robert came with me. But nothing happend and then it was time to go eat. And so I asked my mom if Robert could eat at our house and she said OK. But Robert's mom said he couldn't because she made spaghetty all day. Which Robert likes quite a bit anyway. And so do I. So I asked my mom if I could eat at Robert's and she said GO ASK YOUR DAD. And my dad said NO. So I didn't. So after supper Robert came down and asked my mom if I could sleep at his house like I do sometimes on Saturday. And she said GO ASK YOUR DAD. And I said DO I HAVE TO? And she said YES. And he said NO. And I really wanted to because we have more fun up there. Because his mom always gets drunk on Saturday night and so we could stay up REAL late. But my dad didn't let me like he usually don't. And he wouldn't let Robert stay at my house either. He said we always giggle and make too much noise. And I said PLEASE? And he said YOU HEARD ME! And so I had to stay home all alone and wait, Superman.

But it didn't happen.

I stayed up REAL late but nobody flew through my window who looked like me. I kept waiting and waiting. And then my dad made me turn out all the lights and I still kept waiting. And waiting. And then I fell asleep even though I didn't want to. I couldn't help it because I was real tired from climbing allover the Duck Rock. And that's when it happened, Superman.

I had this dream.

I dreamed I was flying through the air and I was flying real fast and I broke through the Time Barrier. Only I wasn't flying backwords into the past. I was flying forword, into the future.

Like you do sometimes.

And you'll never guess where I landed? I landed right where I

*am write now! Right on top of my dad's apartment building! And it
was late at night. Real late. But my light was still on so I looked in
the window and you'll never guess who I saw?*

It was me, Superman.

*Only I was a LOT bigger. And I was writing a letter to you, just
like this one. Lots of short sentences. Lots of short paragraphs. Only
I wasn't writing it because I was typing it. And I don't even have a
typewriter but that's what I was doing.*

I watched for a long time.

*I looked through the window and I looked at myself and I knew
it was me. I KNEW it! Except I was bigger, like I told you. And I was
crying. Tears kept falling allover my typewriter. The one I don't have
yet. And each tear was a different color. Red and blue and yellow.
And gold. And green, like Kryptonite. They fell everywhere. Rivers
of rainbows flooding the room, getting higher and deeper, attacking
me, drowning me—killing me!*

*It was AWFUL, Superman! I thought FOR SURE I was gonna
die! I kept trying to make it to the window, to pull it open and save
myself. But I couldn't. Somebody was stopping me. Somebody was
outside holding it shut. And that's when it happened, Superman.*

I woke up.

Everybody else was asleep. Even Buster. I wished
Robert was there so I could tell him about that dream, but
he wasn't. He'd been gone a long time. I was all alone. It
was the middle of the night. I was still crying. Still
writing. Still waiting for someone who looks like me to fly
through the window and dry my tears and pick me up and
fly away. Will it ever happen, Superman?

Will it ever happen?

just,
Jerry

I'll tell you, SUPERMAN,

It sure is hard to figure this all out. But me and Robert hardly ever give up and that's why we're still trying. So we've been thinking about how Ma and Pa Kent died a long time ago and you felt real bad and cryed and everything. So maybe that's why you don't want to fly back through the Time Barrier and ask them about Saint Clark. Because you'd know they're already dead only they wouldn't know it and so you'd have to feel bad all alone.

Except Robert said if you kept flying back into the past then you could be with them ALL the time, Superman. Which means they would NEVER be dead.

And since everybody used to be alive sometime, then you could visit anybody anytime. Not just Ma and Pa Kent, but Abraham Lincoln or Adam and Eve or ANYBODY. And so actually nobody must ever be dead. It's just a matter of getting to them at the right time. Which means all you have to be is Super. Or else you have to be God.

Which might be the same thing anyway.

> Your PALS,
> JERRY and ROBERT

You see, SUPERMAN,

On page 13 of Robert's Catechism it says that GOD IS EVERYWHERE. And on page 14 it says that GOD CAN SEE EVERYTHING. And on page 15 it says that GOD ALWAYS WAS AND HE ALWAYS WILL BE AND HE ALWAYS REMAINS THE SAME. And every time Sister

Mary Justin talks about God it sure sounds like she's talking about you, Superman.

Especially since you can be a man or a boy or a nothing, depending on which time you do it. Which means you can be EVERYWHERE and EVERYWHEN all at the same time. Just like God the Father.

Which is what Robert said a LONG time ago when we first started thinking about it. So now we're thinking about it again because of what Sister Mary Justin keeps saying. And she knows a lot about God just like we know a lot about you, Superman. Except we don't know if you're God or not. So why don't you tell us like you didn't before?

Thank you very much.

ROBERT and JERRY

———✦———

DEAR MAN OF STEEL,

I figure when I get SUPER then I'll be able to do what you do. Which means that I can be everywhen all at once too. Which means I might also be God if you're God. Except Sister Mary Justin said there's only ONE God so maybe I might be The Baby Jesus. Because he's also God even if there's only one God. Which I don't really understand yet but there's LOTS of things I don't understand yet.

But if I get Super like you then FOR SURE I'll be able to fly into the past and be The Baby Jesus. Which means I might of done it already. Which means I might be The Baby Jesus right now only I don't know it yet. And I'd sure like to be the Son of God if you're God, Superman. But if you're not then I don't want to be either. And if I REALLY am The

Baby Jesus, then do you think my mom is The Virgin Mary?

> Your friends,
> JERRY AND ROBERT again

DEAR SUPER-FRIEND,

The other day my mom found my latest SUPERBOY NO. 191 which was hid in my notebook. And I thought she was gonna get mad because I was reading about Superman again. But she didn't. She got mad because I bought it at Bacchio's News Stand. Which is what I told her when she said WHERE DID YOU GET THIS? And then she said DON'T YOU DARE BUY A COMICBOOK THERE EVER AGAIN! And she was really yelling. And I said CAN I BUY SOME BUBBLEGUM? And she said I could never buy NOTHING there ever again as long as I live. And I said WHAT IF I DIDN'T BUY NOTHING? WHAT IF I JUST TALKED TO MRS. BACCHIO? And that's when she REAL-LY got mad, Superman. And she told me how Mrs. Bacchio was a EVIL WOMAN and how she's LIVING IN SIN and how I should NEVER talk to her ever again.

And I said BUT I LIKE MRS. BACCHIO A HOLE LOT!

And she said YOU BETTER LISTEN TO ME YOUNG MAN!

And I said WHY?

And she said BECAUSE I SAID SO!

And I said WHAT IF I DON'T? and so she hit me. And she said that's just a SAMPLE of what I'm gonna get if she ever catches me in Bacchio's ever again. And then she called Elizabeth Sipanno on the telephone. And so now Robert isn't allowed in Bacchio's either. And Robert asked his mom WHY? and she said BECAUSE PEOPLE MIGHT TALK.

And he said ABOUT WHAT? and she said YOU'RE TOO YOUNG TO UNDERSTAND.

And he said IT ISN'T FAIR! and she said DO AS YOU'RE TOLD!

So now we're gonna have to go to Starita's. Which is a drugstore. Which is the only other place that sells comicbooks. Which we don't like very much because Mr. Starita keeps yelling at us and telling us to hurry up and how he don't like kids hanging around his store all the time. Which is why you GOTTA do something, Superman. Because Mrs. Bacchio is the only groan up we REALLY like but she's the only groan up the other groan ups really hate. Because we don't know why yet.

ROBERT and JERRY CHARIOT

———————

Dear Superman,

You know what I don't think? I don't think my mom's The Virgin Mary. Because a Virgin is a woman who finds out she's gonna have a baby before she gets merried. And the way she finds out is that a angel tells her while she's down on her knees praying. That's what me and Robert Sipanno think. But we're not too sure because Bruno who is Robert's big brother wouldn't tell us. He said we're too little to find out about Virgins. Just like we're too little to find out about queers and Mrs. Bacchio and stuff like that. And then the angel tells her that she's supposed to go out and find a husband like Saint Joseph. Because women aren't allowed to have babys all by themselves. Because we don't know why. Not exactly. But we think it's because babys are supposed to have fathers to hit them. And so if a woman has a baby who don't have a father then everybody talks about her.

Especially Veronica nextdoor.

And you know what I don't think, Superman? I don't think the sin is having the baby. I think the sin is not having the father. Or not having a angel to tell you who the father is gonna be. Or something like that. And so I decided to ask my mom about babys and who makes them and allthat. And I didn't even care that Veronica was still there. And my mom said that God does. Which is what Sister Mary Justin said. So I said WELL, DOES GOD PUT THEM IN YOUR STOMICK?

And that's when my mom looked at me like she was gonna be mad. And then she took a deep breath. And then she looked at me like she wasn't gonna be mad. And then she said YES, HE DOES.

And I said WELL HOW DO YOU KNOW?

And she said WHAT DO YOU MEAN?

And I said WHO TOLD YOU THAT GOD PUT A BABY IN YOUR STOMICK? WAS IT A ANGEL? THAT'S HOW THE VIRGIN MARY FOUND OUT, YOU KNOW.

And she looked at Veronica and sort of smiled. And then she said WELL I WOULDN'T EXACTLY CALL IT A ANGEL. And Veronica burst out laughing. A lot. And then Veronica said BUT IT SURE WAS HEAVEN. And then they both started laughing. And I said I DON'T UNDERSTAND. And Veronica said YOU'RE NOT SUPPOSED TO. And my mom said WE'LL TALK ABOUT IT LATER. And so that means we're NEVER supposed to talk about it ever again.

But I wonder what she did see if it wasn't a angel? And so does Robert. And so we hope you'll tell us this time. Thank you.

Your pal,
JERRY CHARIOT

PS: When I get to be God you know what I'm gonna do first? I'm gonna get rid of Hell by using my Super-breath to blow out all the flames. And then I'll take all the people in Hell and fly them to Purgatory because I don't think ANY-BODY'S that bad that they should stay in Hell. Except maybe Buster and Sister Mary Justin and Veronica next-door. And Olivia Mariotti and Jimmy Sinceri and Old Lady Holbrook. And maybe my mom. And so maybe we should have a special place for them. What do you think?

J.C. again

———⬦———

Dear SUPERMAN,

The other day I went to visit my sister the nunn who lives in Erie, Pencilvania, with all the other nunns who aren't really nunns yet. They're kinda like cub scouts who want to be boy scouts but they can't yet. And that's why I can only go there once every four months for two hours in the afternoon sometimes. And so can my mom and my dad and Buster and my baby brother who isn't even borned yet. He gets in with my mom. And we have to sit in a big garden where all the familys of all the other almost-nunns have to sit with us. Except they sit by themselfs on their own benchs. And we have to talk REAL quiet because all the older nunns are inside praying and himing. It sounds just like a hospitel which is where you go when you want to see everybody who's sick. Except nunns aren't sick. They're holy. And they make you stay in the garden and you can NEVER go inside unless you have to pee.

Which usually I do.

So we have to tip-toe so we don't bother anybody. And when you get inside everything's so quiet that you can hear your tip-toes squeeking on the floor. Which is all shiny because nunns must clean all the time except when they're praying. Which is most of the time. And if you sneeze like I did once then it sounds REAL LOUD. I thought it was gonna knock over all the statues. That's why I really hate peeing there, Superman. Because it's so quiet that everybody who's waiting outside can hear you. And there are LOTS of people waiting in line because there's only one place for regular people to pee in the hole place. So I try to pee on the side of the toilet so it don't hit the water because I don't like to make noise when I pee when everybody's listening. Especially nunns.

And also priests.

Priests are around all the time because somebody has to give the nunns Holy Communion when they want it. Which is everyday. Which is what my sister the Sister said. And she also said they go to confession every morning. And I said WHY?

And she said BECAUSE NUNNS HAVE SINS TOO.

And I said REALLY?

And she said OF COURSE, WE'RE HUMAN TOO.

And I said WHAT KINDS OF SINS DO NUNNS HAVE SINCE YOU'RE PRAYING ALL THE TIME?

And she said ONLY GOD KNOWS THAT.

And I said CAN'T YOU TELL ME JUST ONE?

And she said YOU CAN ONLY TELL GOD AND PRIESTS.

And I said BUT YOU CAN TELL ME.

And she said NO I CAN'T.

And I said BUT IF I WAS GOD THEN YOU COULD TELL ME, COULDN'T YOU?

And she said BUT YOU'RE NOT GOD.

And I said WELL I MIGHT BE THE BABY JESUS.

And BOY did she get mad, Superman! REALLY mad! But I can't tell you about it right now because I'm supposed to do my homework before I take my bath. Which is just before I go to bed. So goodby for now. And goodnight.

LOVE,
JERRY CHARIOT

Good morning, SUPERMAN.

The reason I'm writing this letter is because everybody else is still asleep except me. Because I woke up REAL early because I couldn't stop thinking about my sister the Sister who gets up at 5 o'clock to pray before she goes to the bathroom or it gets light out. And then she goes to the chapel and prays some more before she gets her Holy Communion. Which is after she went to confession. And then she goes to the cafeteria where she has to pray before she can eat. And then she eats. And then she prays some more to thank God she finished eating. And then she reads the Bible after she sings some hims and salms. Which was before she waxed the floors because it was her turn. And after that she meditates. And I said WHAT DOES THAT MEAN?

And she said I THINK ABOUT GOD AND HOW I CAN LOVE HIM SOME MORE AND IF I'M HOLY ENOUGH TO SERVE HIM.

And I said YOU SEEM PRETTY HOLY TO ME.

And then she eats lunch after she thanks God she's gonna eat lunch. And then it's afternoon and so it starts allover again. And so what I wanted to know was where she finds the time to commit all those sins. But she wouldn't tell me. Not even when I said I might be The Baby Jesus. Which is when the hole thing started. Which I'll have to tell you about later because my mom's coming up the steps to wake me up. Goodby.

JERRY again

Hello, Superman.

The reason I know all that stuff about how she prays and everything is because that's what she always talks about when we sit in the garden with all the flowers and statues and nunns and things. And she always asks the same questions like HOW'S ANT HELLEN? and HOW'S JERRY DOING IN SCHOOL? And that's when I said I HAVE TO GO TO THE BATHROOM. And she said she would have to go inside with me because I wasn't allowed to go inside alone. Which I already knew. So I figured if I took a poop then it would be almost time to go back to Pulpburg and she couldn't hear about school. But there was a hole bunch of other people standing in line and I wondered if they really had to poop like I didn't. So I peed.

And on the way back she asked me if I liked Sister Mary Justin. And I said SORTA.

And she said Sister Mary Justin was one of the BEST nunns in the hole convent. And I said ARE YOU SURE?

And she said she hadn't seen Sister Mary Justin in a long time but she couldn't wait till Sister Mary Justin comes to Erie again so she could find out all about me.

And I said WHEN DO YOU THINK THAT WILL BE?

And she said SOON I HOPE.

And I said REAL SOON?

And she said MAYBE.

So I said CAN I ASK YOU SOMETHING REAL IMPORTENT?

And she said OF COURSE again.

And I said PROMISE YOU WON'T TELL ANYBODY ABOUT IT? NOT EVEN SISTER MARY JUSTIN?

And she said IF YOU WANT.

And I said WELL, HAVE YOU EVER HEARD OF SUPERMAN?

And she said YOU MEAN THE COMICBOOK?

And I said AND ALSO ON TV.

And she said OF COURSE I HAVE.

And I said DO YOU LIKE HIM?

And she said WELL I GUESS SO.

And I said DO YOU BELIEVE HE EXISTS LIKE GOD EXISTS?

And she said GOOD AFTERNOON, SISTER MONICA.

And Sister Monica said GOOD AFTERNOON, SISTER.

And they both smiled like all nunns smile. Which is just like all the statues in the garden smile. Except not many of the statues are smiling because they're mostly praying. Which is when my mom came over and we started talking about how nunns have sins. Which I'll have to tell you about later because Robert's waiting for me. We have to go up Old Lady Holbrook's and practice my flying because today's Wednesday. Yesterday was Tuesday so I worked on my X-ray Vision. Except I'll have to tell you about that later also. So long.

Your Friends,
JERRY and ROBERT

———————

Dear Superman,

I think you're God and Robert thinks you're God but nobody else does. Especially my mom and my dad and my sister the Sister who is becoming a nunn almost. She doesn't even think you're Superman or anything. In fact she doesn't believe in you at all. And she doesn't believe in me either. She said that God is God and Jesus is God and that's it. Except for the Holy Ghost. She said that you're not God and I'm not Jesus and WHERE HAVE YOU BEEN GETTING THESE NOTIONS? And I said I FIGURED IT OUT ALL BY MYSELF AND ROBERT. And she just looked at me. And the way she looked at me was the same way that Sister Mary Justin in school looks at me. That's how I knew she was gonna be a good nunn for sure.

Anyway, my mom got REAL mad. Almost as mad as my dad did. Buster didn't do nothing because he was writing a postcard to Mary Louise that he bought at Howard Johnson's. And I could tell my dad was gonna hit me but my sister the Sister wouldn't let him. She said I was just a little mixed up. And my dad said WAIT TILL I GET HIM HOME, I'LL STRAIGHTEN HIM OUT! And that's when we had to leave because all the nunns had to go pray again. And my sister told my dad how she would talk to me next time we went to Erie and she would straighten me out so my dad wouldn't have to do it. But I could tell he was gonna do it anyway. And I was right. All the way back to Pulpburg he didn't even talk once while he was driving. Not even to my mom.

And it took three hours to get home.

And when we got out of the car he didn't even wait till we got in the house or anything. He just grabbed me by the ankles and he held me up in the air with his hand and he kept hitting me and hitting me. And I had a bunch of pennys in my pocket which fell allover the sidewalk while he was hitting me and while my mom was yelling STOP IT STOP IT YOU'LL KILL THE BOY! And even my mom was crying like I was. And my dad was yelling how he'll break my leg if I ever do that again NOW GET IN THE HOUSE AND GET TO BED BEFORE I DO IT RIGHT NOW! And I could hardly even walk inside because it was really hurting and I was really crying and my mom and dad kept yelling for a long time after I went to bed. I could hear them fighting all the way upstairs and my dad said THERE'S SOMETHING WRONG WITH THE KID!

And my mom said YOU DON'T HAVE TO BEAT HIM LIKE THAT!

And my dad said I'LL DO WHAT I DAMN WELL PLEASE!

And my mom said FOR CHRIST'S SAKE!

And my dad said SHUT UP BEFORE I HIT YOU TOO!

And my mom started to say something and my dad hit her. Real hard. I couldn't see it but BOY could I hear it. And then I heard my mom crying for a long time and then my dad went out and slammed the door. He was probly going to the Italien Club because that's where he always goes when he wants to be alone with the boys.

And then it was 2 o'clock in the morning and he still didn't come back yet and my mom was still crying and

106

waiting downstairs. That's why I couldn't sleep. Because I really hate him, Superman. I hate him more than Luthor or The Joker or Jimmy Sinceri or ANYBODY. Even Sister Mary Justin. Because I don't care if you're God or not, Superman. And I don't care if I'm God or not. I don't care about anything except getting Super. And getting even. And if he ever hits my mom again then I'll get a knife. And I'll stick it in him when he's snoring. I swear to God I'll do it! And I know you hardly ever hurt or kill anybody but I don't care, Superman. Because I just don't. Because you'll see.

JERRY CHARIOT

DEAR SUPERMAN,

Robert said you NEVER kill anybody and I said you might if you really had to. And Robert said Well you ain't never killed anybody yet. And I said ARE YOU SURE? So we looked in all our old comicbooks and also the two new ones we bought at Starita's. And we couldn't even find one place where you killed somebody even though everybody is trying to kill you all the time. And I didn't mean it when I said I was gonna kill my dad. I was just kidding. Ha-Ha. I would never REALLY kill him. I just want to get rid of him for a while. Like maybe he'll get sick and have to go in the hospitel or something. That's all. Ha-Ha.

Your Friend,
JERRY

PS: The other day we was on our way to the Duck Rock and we saw this rock on the ground and I looked at it a LONG time and then I told Robert there was Kryptonite inside of it. And Robert said HOW DO YOU KNOW? And I said BECAUSE I CAN SEE IT WITH MY X-RAY VISION. And Robert said I DON'T BELIEVE YOU. So we broke it open and guess what? There was this green stuff inside and it was Kryptonite. We think. Except I'm sure of it. And so we burried it in the ground just in case. You're welcome.

———⊷⊶———

DEAR SUPERPAL,

Me and Robert just read the story about how The Kryptonite Kid came from another planet and tried to kill you with his dog and his Kryptonite touch in GIANT SUPERBOY NO. 10. And he kept turning everything into Kryptonite, even the trees and the sliding boards and Krypto's bones. And he told you if you didn't leave Earth forever then he'd kill you FOR SURE and his Kryptonite dog would also kill Krypto. But you couldn't kill him first because every time you got near him you got weak and started to die. And besides, you wouldn't kill him anyway because that's just the way you are. And on page 33 he turned the chairs and the books and the floor and everything into Kryptonite. And he said,

"HOW ABOUT A KRYPTONITE ASH TRAY? OH, YOU DON'T SMOKE? THEN AMUSE YOURSELF WITH A KRYPTONITE PHONE BOOK!"

And then you said, "OWWW! HE'S CHANGING HARMLESS OBJECTS INTO DEADLY MENACES!"

And me and Robert thought you was a gonner for sure this time. And so did you, Superman. You was laying on the floor and starting to turn all green and your forehead was real sweaty. And The Kryptonite Kid was laughing and saying,

"TRY TO GET UP! JUST TRY! HA-HA! MY DOG AND I HAVE CHANGED OURSELVES INTO KRYPTONITE! YOU WOULDN'T LEAVE EARTH, DESPITE MY WARNING, SO NOW YOU MUST DIE!"

And you said, "THE PAIN . . . GHASTLY . . ."

And we was REALLY AFRAID, Superman. We was so afraid that we couldn't even turn the page. So we decided to flip a coin and Robert lost. Except he said maybe we better say a prayer first and this way everything would turn out allright.

But I said it wouldn't make no difference anyway because whatever was gonna happen had already happend.

Except Robert said maybe God had looked into the future to see if we was gonna do it. And if we WAS gonna say a prayer for Superman then maybe he would make everything come out OK because that's the way God works sometimes.

So finally we decided to say three Hail Marys just in case. And also one Our Father Who Art In Heaven. Then we both put a hand on the page and turned it together, Superman. And that's when somebody came to save you just in time Thank God and you'll NEVER guess who it was?

It was MXYZPTLK!—the prank-playing imp from The Fifth Dimension!

"YOU BET IT'S ME!" the imp said. "YOU OUTWITTED ME THE LAST TIME WE MET, REMEMBER, AND I VOWED TO GET EVEN, YOU SUPER-CRUMB, YOU!"

And then Mr. Mxyzptlk! used his magical powers to send The Kryptonite Kid to The Fifth Dimension where he couldn't kill you anymore. And then he changed everything back to normel so there wouldn't be anymore Kryptonite around for a while. And you couldn't figure out why he did it because you thought he HATED you, Superman.

Which he does.

And so if you was dead then he couldn't make you miserable anymore. And then he wouldn't have anymore fun.

So it's a GOOD thing he hates you so much because he don't hate you as much as The Kryptonite Kid did. And that's why you better be nice to Mr. Mxyzptlk! and let him torment you for a while. Because if The Kryptonite Kid ever excapes from The Fifth Dimension then you're gonna need all the help you can get.

So goodby.

                          YOUR FRIENDS,
                          JERRY and ROBERT

PS: Maybe you should change your mind about killing people. Because someday somebody's gonna kill you unless you kill them first. It's OK if you kill somebody as long as they try to kill you before you try to kill them. That's what me and Robert think. So why don't you think about it also? Please.

———————

DEAR MR. MXYZPTLK!

I hope you don't mind if me and Robert Sipanno write you a letter but we just wanted to say THANK YOU VERY MUCH for saving Superman's life from The Kryptonite Kid. We thought that was REAL nice. And we know how you hate to be nice but we still like you quite a bit anyway. So if you ever decide to come to Pulpburg then you don't have to worry about spelling your name backwords. We promise we won't trick you. So THANK YOU VERY MUCH again.

> Your Friends,
> MR. CHARIOT! and MR. SIPANNO!

PS: We hope this letter gets to you OK because we don't know if the mailman delivers letters to The Fifth Dimension or not. In fact, we don't even know where The Fifth Dimension is because we live in The Fourth Dimension. I think. But we're gonna send it AIRMAIL just in case. Goodby.

Dear SUPERPAL,

The other day I saw another rock with Kryptonite in it and I told Robert. So we broke it open and I was right again. It was all green inside. And so I looked around some more and I found another one and we cracked it open and it was green also. So now we know why you never fly around Pulpburg—because there's so much Kryptonite around! But don't worry, we'll get rid of it for you and then you can come and see us if you want. And I sure hope there isn't any red or silver or white Kryptonite around. Or gold.

So maybe I better check.

Goodby.

> JERRY CHARIOT
> and ROBERT SIPANNO

PS: You know what Robert said, Superman? Robert said maybe he should call me THE KRYPTONITE KID because I

keep finding Kryptonite allover the place especially near
the Duck Rock. But I said YOU BETTER NOT! and Robert
said WHY? and I said BECAUSE THE KRYPTONITE KID
WAS REAL BAD AND HE TRIED TO KILL SUPERMAN
AND I WOULD NEVER TRY TO KILL NOBODY EXCEPT
MAYBE MY DAD. Except Robert said I could still be THE
KRYPTONITE KID except I'd be a GOOD kid instead of the
REAL kid. So what do you think?

Dear MAN OF STEEL,

Today in church we was practicing how to go to
confession and Sister Mary Justin was pretending she was
the priest. And she said we had to go on the other side of
the booth and tell her ALL our sins just like we're supposed
to tell the REAL priest when we make our First Holy
Confession. Which is why we was practicing. And she told
Janie Jobb to write down anybody's name who talks while
she's in the booth because Janie Jobb ALWAYS gets to do
that. Because she don't even care that everybody HATES
her except Sister Mary Justin. And pretty soon it was my
turn to go in the booth and kneel down on the other side of
the curtain and make the Sign of the Cross and tell her all
the bad stuff I been doing lately. So I decided to put a
handkerchief over my mouth like I saw on TV one time and
this way she wouldn't know it was me and she might think
it's Jimmy Sinceri who's a queer. And she said YOU'RE
WHAT?

And I said MY BROTHER SAID I WAS A QUEER.

And she said DO YOU KNOW WHAT A QUEER IS?

And I said NOT EXACTLY.

And she said WELL YOU BETTER NEVER FIND OUT
BECAUSE IT'S A SIN!

And I said WELL DO YOU THINK I'M A QUEER?

And she said SHUT UP, JEROME!

And I wondered how she knew it wasn't Jimmy.

So I said I GOTTA FIND OUT WHAT A QUEER IS SO I CAN BE CAREFUL IN CASE I MIGHT BECOME ONE.

And she said RETURN TO YOUR PEW, JEROME!

And I said IF I BECOME A QUEER THEN IT'S YOUR FAULT BECAUSE YOU WON'T TELL ME WHAT IT IS AND NEITHER WILL ANYBODY ELSE!

And she didn't say nothing and I could hear her breathing real heavy on the other side of the curtain and so I knew she was mad. That's why I went back to my pew and thought about it for a LONG time. And I decided a sin can't be a sin if you don't know it's a sin. And so a queer can't be a queer if nobody knows he's a queer. Especially if the queer don't know he's a queer. And I wonder how many queers are running around who don't know it? I bet there must be LOTS of them. What do you think, Superman?

> Love,
> JERRY THE KID

PS: When I get SUPER maybe I could put KK on my indestructable outfit instead of S. And I could have a green outfit instead of a blue one like yours. This way everybody wouldn't get us mixed up when they looked up in the sky and said LOOK! UP IN THE SKY! IT'S A BIRD! IT'S A PLANE! NO, IT'S THE KRYPTONITE KID! So what do you think?

———❈———

Dear Superman,

You know what we did? We snuck in Bacchio's and we

told Mrs. Bacchio how she's REAL nice and REAL pretty and we like her a HOLE LOT. And we told her how my mom said that we couldn't ever go in there ever again. And we told her how it wasn't our fault and we'll write her letters if it's OK and here's a pansy which we picked in my mom's garden. And she took the flower and she smiled real pretty and she cryed at the same time. And she grabbed our heads and she rubbed our hair and she put her arms around our shoulders and she cryed some more. Then she gave us two free comicbooks and she said Thank You and she was still crying. And we're the ones who should've said Thank You but we didn't because she said it first. So we said Your Welcome Mrs. Bacchio. Then we left while she was still crying. That's exactly the way it happend.

YOUR PALS,
JERRY AND ROBERT

PS: Robert said the reason you haven't come to talk to Mrs. Bacchio yet was because there might be some Kryptonite around Bacchio's News Stand and that's why we're gonna check it out for you OK? Goodby.

Dear Mrs. Bacchio,
    You're the only person we ever wrote a letter to except for Superman and Lois Lane and Jimmy Olsen and Mr. Mxyzptlk! And the main reason we're writing is because we forgot to tell you how we want you to check around your store for Kryptonite the next time you decide to clean it. And if you find any then maybe you should bury it. And also we wanted to say THANK YOU VERY MUCH for the

comicbooks and also for everything else. Especially everything else.

> Your Friends,
> Jerry Chariot and Robert Sipanno

PS: Say HI to Mr. Durrelli the next time you see him OK?

DEAR MAN FROM KRYPTON,

Well, so far we found sixteen pieces of green Kryptonite and two pieces of red Kryptonite and four pieces of gold Kryptonite and we burried them all. And every time I find another piece of Kryptonite I always wash my hands REAL good after I bury it. That's so I won't get any of it on this letter or any other letter we write. I just thought you might want to know that just in case you're afraid to open our letters sometimes.

> Your Friends,
> THE KRYPTONITE KID and ROBERT

DEAR SUPERMAN,

The other day me and Robert went over to Bacchio's after school because we wanted to check for that Kryptonite. Only we couldn't go inside because my mom said so. So we was checking the outside and you'll never guess who came by? It was my dad. He was beeping the horn and yelling and so Robert went home. But I had to go over to the car because he's my dad. And he said WHAT THE HELL ARE YOU DOING? And I said Robert lost something and I was helping him find it. And I really hated lieing but I really had to. You understand. So my dad made me get in the car and he said he was taking me home. Only he had to stop at the Italien Club first. And I said WHY? And he said BECAUSE IT'S NONE OF YOUR BUSINESS. So when we got to the Italien Club he said I had to wait in the car because he would only be a couple of minutes. So I waited. And waited. And then I started reading my Catechism (which is really Robert's Catechism) because I didn't have any comicbooks with me. And I read QUESTION NO. 4 which is

4. WHAT MUST YOU DO TO BE HAPPY WITH GOD IN HEAVEN?

To be happy with God in Heaven I must know Him, love Him and serve Him in this world. Most of all, I must love Him. We give gifts to those we love. I must make my life a gift to God. I must love God more than I love myself. I must love God more than anybody else. I must love God above all things. It doesn't matter that I can't see Him or feel Him. Or touch him. Or fly with Him, or to Him. Still I must love Him, even if I must hate somebody else because they don't. Because they do things with Mr. Durrelli. Still I must love Him more than myself. My self? HA-HA! Amen.

And I know that's not what it says exactly because it would NEVER say anything like that. But I didn't have anything else to do because my dad was SURE taking a long time, Superman. And I was tired of reading my Catechism and the car radio was broke. And that's why I decided to write you a letter and let you know what happend the other day when Sister Mary Justin wanted to hear some more sins and I said I DON'T HAVE ANY.

And she said WHAT?

And I said I DON'T REALLY KNOW WHAT SINS ARE ANYMORE.

And she said WELL DON'T YOU EVER LIE?

And I said JUST SOMETIMES.

And she said WELL LIEING IS A SIN.

And I said WELL EVERYTIME I TELL THE TRUTH I GET HIT. BUT IF I LIE THEN I DON'T. SO I LIKE LIEING BETTER.

So Sister Mary Justin said WELL GOD DOESN'T, SO YOU BETTER TELL THE TRUTH FROM NOW ON.

So I said OK. But when I said that I lied. This way she'll think I'm telling the truth. But if I told the truth all the time then she'd know how much I lie. And it's better I tell her what she wants to hear than if I tell her the truth. Because then she'll think I'm a good kid. I do what I'm told. I'm sitting in the car waiting. Just waiting. Which is why I've GOT to do something, Superman. Because it's getting dark out and I know my mom will be wondering where I am. Because I was supposed to go dump the garbage a LONG time ago. And it's bad enough my dad's mad at me for being with Robert at Bacchio's. I don't want my mom mad at me for being with my dad at the Italien Club. So I got two choices, Superman: Go in or go home.

So I went in.

My dad was sitting on a stool at the bar. There was only a couple other people inside who were standing beside my dad. Who was sitting. And there was also another person way down at the other end sitting by himself. And singing to himself. But you couldn't hear what he was singing very good because his head was in his arms. And his arms were on the edge of the bar. And the bar looked just like the ones you see in GUNSMOKE all the time on TV. Except nobody was wearing cowboy hats. In fact nobody was wearing any hats at all, except for the man who kept singing and burping. He was wearing a helmet like you wear when you want to build a building. And he also had a lunch bucket next to his elbow on the bar. And there was a bowling machine over in the corner which was making a LOT of noise because somebody was playing with it.

It was Robert's father.

So I just stood by the door and watched everybody for a while. But my dad didn't see me. He was talking to the bar tender who was giving him another beer. So I waited. And nobody saw me yet. So I waited some more. And the man started singing louder. And somebody told him to shut the Hell up. So I started going into the room and that's when the bar tender saw me. So he pointed. And my dad turned around. And so did Robert's father who was bowling. And Robert's father said WELL IF IT ISN'T LITTLE BUSTER. And I really hated that. So he grabbed me by the shoulder and he brought me over to my dad and he picked me up and he put me on a stool. Right next to my dad.

And the bar tender said WHAT'LL IT BE, KID? And everybody laughed. And somebody said GIVE HIM A BEER, SAM! And everybody laughed louder. And my dad's eyes were all red but he wasn't mad. He looked like he didn't feel very good. Somebody poked him on the shoulder and said, HEY, YOUR KID'S LOOKING FOR YOU! And everybody laughed and somebody said WHERE'S YOUR MAMA, KID? HA-HA! And my dad burped. And the man way at the end started laughing and singing real loud. And what he was singing was THERE'S NOoooooooooooooOOOOOOOOOOO PLACE LIKE HOOOOOOOOOOOOOOOOoooooooOOOOOOOOOOOOOOOOME!

HA-HA! So my dad just looked at me. And then he said You better go wait in the car. And everybody laughed again. And somebody said HE'LL BE RIGHT OUT, KID! and everybody laughed louder. And so I walked towards the door and I looked back and everybody waved and laughed. Except my dad. He didn't do nothing. He just sat there.

He didn't come outside for a long time because I waited. And waited. And then I walked home all by myself in the dark. And when I got home my mom was crying again. Only she wasn't mad or anything. Not at me. But she called the Italien Club and they said he wasn't there. But my mom knew he was. Because I told her. But she just said WELL IF HE COMES IN TELL HIM TO COME HOME and she hung up. And then she gave me a sandwich and some milk. And then she said it's time to go to bed. And then she started crying again. She was crying real soft but I could hear her all the way from my bedroom. She cryed for a long time. Until I fell asleep. And then I had another dream.

I dreamed I was walking into a bar that looked just like the Italian Club. Only I wasn't little anymore. I was big. Like my dad. I sat down on a stool and the bar tender said HI'YA, JER and I said HI'YA, SAM and then I said GIMME A BEER and he did. And there was somebody way at the end of the bar who was burping and singing to himself. I couldn't tell who it was, but he looked a lot like Robert Sipanno. Except I wasn't sure because he was wearing a helmet. A soldier's helmet. And his head was in his arms and his arms were on the bar. And so was his gun. He was fingering it mechanically, like rosary beads. So I looked at Sam and I said WHO'S THAT OVER THERE? And Sam said I DUNNO, HE JUST CAME IN OUT OF NOWHERE. So I picked up my beer and I walked down the bar and I stood right next to him. ROBERT? I said. But he didn't look up. ROBERT? IT'S ME—JERRY. He was still sort of singing but he wouldn't look up and that's when he started laughing, high and screechy like a girl, laughing and crying and singing at the same time. So I grabbed his helmet. I started pulling his head up. But allofasudden he jerked around quickly, fiercely—like a bullet he sprang forward and attacked me and I knew it was Robert. I KNEW it! It didn't matter that his face was covered with blood and he didn't have any eyes and there was a statue of the Virgin Mary in his pocket, crying. It didn't matter because nothing mattered.

Because I woke up.

Everything was quiet, Superman. Except for my dad. He was snoring on the couch because my mom locked the bedroom door. And Buster was talking in his sleep like he always does about Mary Louise. So I couldn't go back to sleep.

I tried, but I couldn't.

So I decided to get out a piece of paper and write you a letter about Robert, my BESTfriend. The only person who really understands me and helps me and loves me, Superman.

He says I have X-ray Vision and I can find Kryptonite. BOY can I find it! ALLover the place!

He stands beneath that apple tree and smiles, then laughs as I fly into the sky like a plane, my arms out in front of me, my cape flapping behind me—flying higher, making loops, snatching an apple from the uppermost branch: HERE, ROBERT, CATCH!—then shooting straight up like a rocket, like a streak of light: WATCH THIS, ROBERT! LOOK, ROBERT! I'M FLYYYYYYYYYYYYING!

Now do you understand, Superman? I could fly. I did fly. I CAN fly because Robert's looking up at me. Because Robert believes in me. Because that's all there really is, Superman.

That's all there ever was.

The
Fourth
Dimension

Dear SUPERMAN,

The other day Jimmy Sinceri saw one of my comic-books in my notebook and he grabbed it. And I said YOU BETTER GIVE IT BACK!

And he said I'M GONNA SHOW IT TO SISTER MARY JUSTIN!

And I said YOU BETTER GIVE IT BACK! again.

And he said WHO'S GONNA MAKE ME?

And I said ME!

And he started laughing and so did Duane Machado who flunked the first grade and so he's a lot older than everybody else. And also a lot bigger and fatter and uglier. And Jimmy said he knew FOR SURE there wasn't a real Superman and I was the STUPIDEST kid in the class and maybe I was the STUPIDEST kid in the entire world. And Duane said that Robert Sipanno was the second stupidest kid and they both started laughing again. Robert wasn't around because he was in the lavatory. So I tried to grab the comicbook but I couldn't because they're a LOT bigger than me. Especially Duane who's the biggest person in the class and who pushed me against the wall. Real hard. And so I said YOU JUST WAIT TILL I GET SUPER LIKE SUPERMAN! BOY ARE YOU GONNA GET IT!

And they both started laughing REAL HARD. And Jimmy said WHO'S GONNA GET SUPER—YOU?

And I said ME!

And he said HA-HA!

And I said YOU BETTER STOP IT!

And they both said HA-HA and then Duane pushed me again. So I pushed him back. So he hit me and I hit him and he hit me again and my nose started to bleed when I fell and he kicked me. And Jimmy just watched and laughed. And Duane said IF YOU GET UP I'LL HIT YOU AGAIN! And Jimmy grabbed my comicbook and he tore it up and he threw it allover me and he said SUPERMAN and they both HA-HA'd again. And so now I REALLY hate them and they don't like me either. And neither does a lot of the other kids in school. In fact, just about everybody doesn't like me very much except Robert. And you. And my mom said WHAT HAPPEND TO YOUR NOSE?

And I said I fell.

And she said YOU'RE SO DAM CLUMBSY!

And Robert said it don't matter what everybody else says. Because he's my friend and I'm his friend and we're both your friend, Superman. And there's nobody else we want to be friends with anyway except maybe Jimmy Olsen. Except he don't go to Holy Redeemer School like we have to. So we talked about it a LONG time and we decided when we make our First Holy Communion next month, that's when I'm gonna do it. I'm gonna fly, Superman.

I'm REALLY gonna fly!

I'm gonna jump off the roof of my dad's apartment building so I can get a real good start. And then I'm gonna fly all the way to Holy Redeemer Church and get my First Holy Communion in front of Jimmy Sinceri and Duane Machado and Sister Mary Justin and everybody. Except Robert said maybe I should wait until AFTER we get our First Holy Communion and this way if something goes wrong then I'll go to Heaven for sure. But I told Robert that I want to do it when EVERYBODY'S gonna see me, especially my mom and my dad and Veronica nextdoor. And Buster.

BOY are they gonna be surprised!

LOVE,
JERRY and ROBERT

PS: When I decide what time I'm gonna do it exactly, I'll let you know OK? This way you can come and see it if you want. Or else you could watch it on your X-ray Vision.

DEAR SUPERMAN,

My mom said she's gonna get me a new suit for my First Holy Communion, and so I'm gonna make sure it's a green one. And just before I fly I'm gonna get some chalk and write KK on it. And then I'm gonna borrow my mom's green towel and I'm gonna put it over my shoulders. And then I'm gonna climb up on the roof through the attic window and I'm gonna stand there until somebody sees me. And then I'm gonna wait until a few more people see me. And then I'm gonna put out my arms and bend down and jump up and flyyyyyyyyy all the way across the Clarion River and right to the foot of the altar where I'll stick out my tongue and get my First Holy Communion wafer.

Except Robert said maybe I shouldn't fly off my dad's roof. Maybe I should fly off a wall or something. But I said the reason I can't fly very far right now is because I gotta be higher up. Just like you, Superman. You're ALWAYS jumping out of windows and stuff all the time and you're not afraid of falling. And so neither am I. And I figure the

only way I'm ever gonna do it is if I do it. And besides, I
KNOW I can do it because I REALLY hate Jimmy Sinceri
and I'll show everybody. I will. You'll see.

Goodby.

THE KRYPTONITE KID
and ROBERT SIPANNO

PS: I figure I'll be doing it about 10:30 in the morning
because Sister Mary Justin said Mass starts at 11. And it's
not this Sunday and it's not next Sunday because it's the
Sunday after that. So don't forget to remember.

⊶⊷

Dear MAN of STEEL,

This afternoon we had to go to church like we always
do so we could confess our sins to Sister Mary Justin. And
every time we walk over to the church we have to stand in
line like soldiers and we aren't allowed to talk to NOBODY
because Sister Mary Justin keeps walking up and down
the line to check on us. And if she sees us talking, then
she'll pretend that she didn't see us talking until it's our
turn to go into the booth. Which is when we're supposed to
confess it before she does or else we're in REAL trouble,
Superman.

That's why I don't like to talk when we walk over to
church and Robert walks right beside me like he always
does. And usually Stephen Lins walks right behind me but
when Stephen got the mumps that meant that Jimmy
Sinceri got to be right behind me. And since Jimmy don't
like me very much anyway he decided to poke me in the
back and whisper names when Sister Mary Justin wasn't
looking. And Sister Mary Justin likes him a hole lot and so

she hardly ever watches him anyway. So I couldn't do nothing back because I couldn't turn around because she might see me. So I kept walking and he kept poking and then he whisperd STUPID real loud and a couple people giggled. And Sister Mary Justin said WHAT'S GOING ON DOWN THERE? And nobody said nothing.

And a little while later Jimmy took out his fountain pen and he was gonna squirt it on the back of my shirt. Only I didn't know it then. I found out later when Robert reached out and grabbed it real quick. And Jimmy whisperd GIMME MY NEW PEN BACK! And Robert didn't say nothing. So Jimmy spitted on the back of Robert's neck. And Robert didn't do nothing. So Jimmy whisperd how he's gonna punch Robert's lights out after school SO GIMME MY PEN BACK! So you know what Robert did, Superman? He pretended he was gonna hand it to Jimmy but then he handed it to me instead. And then I dropped it down a drain in the road in front of Holy Redeemer Church where he could NEVER get it back. Wasn't that good Ha-Ha?

Love,
JERRY and ROBERT

PS: You should have seen me after school, Superman! Jimmy chased me and Duane chased me and NOBODY could catch me. So I ran all the way up Old Lady Holbrook's and I climbed the tree and I jumped right away. BOY did I jump! I couldn't believe it. I NEVER went that far before. And it was real easy. You should have seen me, Superman. You should have SEEN me!

Love again,
THE KRYPTONITE KID

PS: Robert saw me.

DEAR SUPERMAN,

The other day Sister Mary Justin was teaching us how to write poems and stuff like that. She said a poem was just a bunch of words except they rhime. I thought it was spelt rime but Robert said there's a H in it. And Sister Mary Justin said you're supposed to write poems about people you love. That's why a lot of people write poems about God and Virgins and stuff like that. And then she told us to go home and write a poem for our homework. And she said it should be about somebody we love a LOT like our mom or the Pope. And she said we're not supposed to get help from anybody not even Robert. So here's what I wrote and Robert didn't help me at all and it goes like this:

> ROSES ARE RED
> AND BUSTER LIKES TOAST.
> I LOVE YOU JESUS
> AND ALSO THE HOLY GHOST. AMEN.

So how do you like it?

> Your friend,
> JERRY CHARIOT

PS: I told Robert we should write a poem about you because we love you more than God or anybody. But Sister Mary Justin don't. That's why I decided I better write about God this time and I could write about you next rhime. So I hope you don't mind.

Dear SUPERPAL,

After school we went shopping and my mom told me how I'm gonna look real good in a white suit. And I said WHITE! And she pretended she didn't hear me just like she always doesn't when I say something she don't like. So I said I AIN'T GONNA WEAR NO WHITE SUIT. I HATE WHITE. I WANT A GREEN ONE. And she still didn't say nothing. But when we got to the store she told the man that we was looking for a white suit please. And I said WE AIN'T LOOKING FOR A WHITE SUIT. SHE IS. I WANT A GREEN ONE. And the man looked at me and then he looked at my mom and then he took out a white suit. And when he wasn't looking my mom grabbed my ear and twisted it real hard and whisperd YOU'LL WEAR WHAT I TELL YOU TO WEAR! And when we went in the little room to try it on I felt real dumb because LOTS of other kids was in the store because it looks like just about everybody is getting a white suit for our First Holy Communion. Including me. And Duane Machado saw my mom going in with me and I heard him giggle REAL loud. So when his mom went in with him I giggled even louder so he would be sure to hear me back. And my mom said BE QUIET and she hit me. And that's why people who are mothers should realize that kids ain't always kids. Especially in front of other kids because that's when they become people. So I hope you don't mind if I do it in a white suit instead of a green one. Goodby

                              Your Pal,
                              THE KID AGAIN

PS: Robert said I forgot to tell you and Jimmy Olsen what his poem was and he hopes you like it a HOLE LOT because it goes like this:

> ROSES ARE RED
> AND SO IS MY MOTHER
> EVERY TIME SHE GETS DRUNK
> IN FRONT OF ME AND MY BROTHER.

Isn't that good?

DEAR SUPERFRIEND,

Well, Sister Mary Justin didn't think it was very good. In fact she hated it. And she told Robert he had to take it home and his mother had to sign it and he had to bring it back by Wednesday. In fact she said EVERYBODY should get their poems signed by their moms so they could see it. Or else their dads. So Robert said IS IT OK IF YOUR BIG BROTHER SIGNS IT? And Sister Mary Justin said NO ROBERT! She really doesn't like Robert a hole lot. Almost as much as his poem. Which she HATED. But she liked mine quite a bit for a change. Especially the AMEN at the end even if it didn't rhyme very good. She still thought it was a REAL good idea to put it there. And then she said we should write another one by Friday and it could be about anybody we wanted. And so I said ANYBODY? And she said YES, JEROME, ANYBODY. And so as soon as I do it I'll send it to you and I hope you like it as much as I'm gonna. So long.

LOVE,
Jerry Chariot and Robert

Dear SUPERMAN,

After school we went in Bacchio's because I don't write as slanted as groan ups do. But Mr. Bacchio said that Mrs. Bacchio wasn't there and Robert said WHERE'D SHE GO? and Mr. Bacchio said she wasn't feeling very good.

So Robert said MAYBE I COULD GO VISIT HER AT HOME BECAUSE TOMORROW'S WEDNESDAY AND I GOTTA SEE HER REAL QUICK.

But Mr. Bacchio said she didn't want to see nobody right now. And even her telephone was disconnected. And she was NEVER gonna sell comicbooks no more and so you better get home boys because he was closing up early from now on.

That's why Robert decided to write his poem for Friday RIGHT AWAY because this way his mom could sign both of them at the same time. It's called "AMEN."

> ROSES ARE RED
> AND FRECKLES ARE PINK
> AND I LOVE MY MOM
> MORE THAN SHE THINKS.
> AMEN. AMEN. AMEN. AMEN. AMEN.

Maybe that'll help.

> Love,
> ROBERT SIPANNO and JERRY

Dear SUPERman,

The other day my brother Buster was sitting on the

couch with Mary Louise. You know who Mary Louise is, don't you? She's the girl my brother always sits on the couch with a BIG nose when nobody's looking. And my mom was in the kitchen making me wash the dishes so I couldn't watch them like I usually can't. Because every time Mary Louise comes over to sit on the couch my mom makes me do something so I can't bother them. Only sometimes I peek when they're not looking. Which is all the time because they keep looking at each other. And sometimes they rub their noses together. Which looks pretty dumb especially since they both got pretty big noses. But the other day they weren't doing that. And they weren't giggling like they usually do all the time. So I KNEW something was wrong.

And so did my mother.

That's why she peeked in and started yelling. And then she started crying while she was still yelling. And then she called Mary Louise's mom and kept whispering about what a EVIL daughter she had. And then my dad came home from work and I heard her whisper how Buster was petting Mary Louise Wesson and he had a erection. And I don't know what a erection is but I know what a erector set is because I got one. That's what you make things out of with. And I also know what petting is because I pet pets all the time. And so does everybody else except my dad. He hates them. That's why nobody who lives in his castle is allowed to have one. Especially me. Because one time I asked him and he said I could have a goldfish. And I said A GOLDFISH? And he said OR ELSE GUPPYS. And I said I DON'T WANT GUPPYS! I WANT PUPPYS! But he said they make too much noise and they poop everywhere. And so I don't know why mom got so mad at Buster again but I'll probly figure it out after I get my Super branes. Which should be about the same time I fly. Which is just a couple weeks away. So don't forget.

Your friends,
JERRY CHARIOT and ROBERT

Dear MAN of TOMORROW,

Well, today's Friday and I just got it finished this morning and it's called "TO SUPERMAN" and I hope you like it because it goes like this:

ROSES ARE RED
YOUR OUTFIT IS BLUE
I LIKE YOU BETTER
THAN JESUS THE JEW. AMEN.

So don't forget to let me know if you like it. Goodby.

YOUR FRIEND,
JERRY CHARIOT AGAIN

PS: And then I'll let you know if Sister Mary Justin likes it OK? Goodby again.

Well, SUPERPAL,

You'll NEVER guess what my brother Buster was doing to Mary Louise on the couch in the living room the other day after school which I already told you about? Well, he wasn't petting her hair which is what I thought. He was petting her tits. That's what Buster said. And I said what's a TITS? And he said A TIT IS A WOMAN'S BREST. And I said BUT MARY LOUISE DON'T EVEN HAVE ANY BRESTS HARDLY. And he said DON'T YOU TALK ABOUT MARY LOUISE THAT WAY! And I said WELL SHE DON'T. And he said YOU BETTER SHUT UP! And I didn't and so he hit me. Real hard. Right in the head. And I just can't figure it out, Superman? Why would Buster want to pet Mary Louise's brests? I mean tits. I think it would be nicer to pet her head and this way you could pretend it's a dog. If you have a dog. Which I don't yet. But I thought as soon as I get Super and fly to Metropolis then maybe I could get one. And I could call him NITE. And then when your dog and my dog played together, we could yell HERE, KRYPTO NITE! Isn't that good?

Your Pal,
JERRY

PS: I want you to know that was my idea and not Robert Sipanno's.

———

Bad news, SUPERMAN.

Remember that poem I wrote which I called "TO SU-PERMAN" which Sister Mary Justin hasn't read yet? Well, she read it. And she hated it even more than I thought she would. And believe me, I thought she was REALLY gonna hate it. And I was right. She hated it so much that she didn't even hit me. She just told me to get out of her sight. She said she NEVER wanted to look at me again. She said to get out, out of this classroom, out of this school, RIGHT THIS INSTANT!

And it was only 9 o'clock in the mourning.

So I waited outside behind the church all day until the bell rang or else my mom would've asked me why I was home so early. And when Robert came out we walked home together like we usually do and he said that Sister Mary Justin said that she was gonna call my mom and dad on the telephone. Tonight after supper. Which she'll probly do FOR SURE because that's the way she is, Superman. Which I'll have to tell you about later because my mom just yelled up the steps it's time to go eat supper. So I'll have to let you know what happens after it happens. Which should be pretty soon. So goodby for now.

JERRY CHARIOT

DEAR SUPERMAN,

It ain't easy being a kid like I and Robert am. I mean is. Especially when your dad and Sister Mary Justin are gonna talk on the telephone any minute now. Because we just finished supper and that's why I'm waiting for the phone to ring. So I was thinking maybe you should let your Superdog Krypto know about how I'm gonna fly on the Sunday after next Sunday at 10:30 in the mourning. This way he could watch it on his X-ray Vision like you're gonna do. Aren't you? Because after it's over I thought FOR SURE I'd fly to Metropolis to visit you for a while. Unless you're already in Pulpburg visiting me. Which you probly won't be since you never even write me letters. I know how busy you are. I wouldn't blame you if you didn't come anyway because I don't like it very much here either. And neither does Robert Sipanno. So I hope you don't mind if I give him a ride to Metropolis with me. He could always stay with Jimmy Olsen if there wasn't room at your place. Besides, I don't think anybody around here is gonna like me very much after I do it. Especially Sister Mary Justin. Because I thought about it a LONG time and I decided when I fly into church to get my First Holy Communion, that's when I'm gonna spit on her. Right on her veil. And if I don't do that, then I'm gonna pee on her head. I SWEAR I will! Because I really HATE her because I'm scared, Superman. I'm sitting in my room waiting. And praying. And wishing the phone wasn't ringing right now. But it is! And my dad just answerd it. And I better sneak over and listen. So goodby.

JERRY

⊷≋⊶

Hello, Superman.

That wasn't Sister Mary Justin Thank God. It was Mr. Marinaro up the street who wanted my dad to go play poker with him at the Italien Club. But my mom said he couldn't go unless he wanted to sleep on the couch again. Which he didn't. Which is why he's in a REAL bad mood already. Which isn't gonna help when Sister Mary Justin calls pretty soon. Because every time my dad gets mad at my mom then he gets mad at me too because I'm HER kid. And then my mom gets mad at me because I'm HIS kid. And then Buster gets mad at me because they get mad at him because he's THEIR kid. What they don't understand is that I'm not ANYBODY's kid, Superman. I'm

THE KRYPTONITE KID

DEAR SUPERMAN,

The reason I didn't write you another letter last night was because I couldn't. Because my dad wouldn't let me. Because Sister Mary Justin said she was gonna show my poem to Father Ponti who is the Pastor of the parish where Holy Redeemer Everything is. And she's gonna ask him to say that I can't get my First Holy Communion until NEXT year because I don't deserve it because I'm the WORST pupil she ever had in her life.

And my dad said WHAT POEM?

So she read it to him REAL loud because even I could hear it. And I was pretty far away from the phone. In fact I was on my way out the door because I didn't want to stick around. But then I rememberd I didn't have my shoes on because I left them in the kitchen with my dad and the telephone. Which is where I wished I didn't take them off. So I snuck back and peeked around the corner and you know what he was doing, Superman?

He was squeezing the phone real hard and he was turning all red and so I thought maybe I could hide in the closet and wait till after he hung up and went to look for me. And then I could sneak in the kitchen and get my shoes and get away. The only trouble was that he didn't hang up. He just dropped the phone while Sister Mary Justin was still talking. And then he started taking off his belt and he yelled JERRY! and I didn't listen and he yelled JERRY! louder and I could tell he really wanted to get me. Which is why I wished I had a knife or something because I figured I was really gonna need it. And I was right. Only I didn't have nothing, Superman. Not even shoes. And so he caught me and hit me again and again and again and again and again and again. And after the seventh time he told me how I have to come STRAIGHT home after school and I can't watch television and I'm not getting ANY more allowence EVER again and I can't play with Robert or anything and I'd be lucky if I was alive when he got through with me.

And then he got through with me.

But I didn't cry this time, Superman. Not until I got up in my room all by myself where nobody could see me. And I got snot allover the sheets and everything but I didn't care because I don't care about NOTHING. Especially him or Sister Mary Justin or ANYBODY. Except Robert. And so I decided I AM gonna kill him, Superman. I AM! And maybe I'll kill Sister Mary Justin too. And maybe I'll kill Veronica nextdoor and Jimmy Sinceri and Duane Machado. Maybe I'll get up in the middle of the night and grab a knife and stick it in them all. Right in their hearts!

> I LOVE YOU, SUPERMAN.
> Jerry

———————✺———————

Dear SUPERPAL,

This morning Sister Mary Justin told everybody in class how she gave my poem to Pastor Ponti and he read it and he didn't like it very much either. In fact he HATED it. But he told Sister Mary Justin how I HAVE TO THINK ABOUT IT FOR A WHILE. And Sister Mary Justin said HOW LONG? And Pastor Ponti said I MUST PRAY FOR GUIDANCE and Sister Mary Justin said WHY? and Pastor Ponti said SO I CAN MAKE THE RIGHT DECISION and

Sister Mary Justin said how she hopes he decides the right conclusion REAL soon. And then she walked right over to my desk. And then she pulled me out of my seat and she said LOOK AT HIM!

And everybody was already looking at me.

And then she said, HE BETTER PRAY HE DON'T DIE BEFORE HE MAKES HIS FIRST HOLY COMMUNION NEXT YEAR! And she talked real loud but she talked real slow and every time she said another word she pulled my hair harder.

HE. BETTER. PRAY. THAT. GOD. DON'T. STRIKE. HIM. *DEAD*!

And when she said *DEAD*! she hit me right on top of my head REAL hard and Jimmy Sinceri laughed. And so did Janie Jobb and Duane Machado and Albert Ambrozzi and Rita Charnovich. And pretty soon the only ones who didn't laugh was me and Robert Sipanno. And when we went to the lavatory later on, Jimmy Sinceri hit me on top of the head just like Sister Mary Justin did. And so did Michael Roinski and a lot of the other guys. And pretty soon even some of the girls started doing it. And so you know what I'm gonna do, Superman? I'm gonna fly in that church and pee on them ALL. On EVERY one of them except Robert. Because I REALLY hate them now, Superman. I really, REALLY hate them!

Your Friend,
THE KID

⚯

Dear MAN OF STEEL,

You know what Pastor Ponti said? He said it's up to

Sister Mary Justin to decide if I don't get my First Holy Communion or not. Because she's my teacher and so she should know. So it looks like I got a new suit for nothing and BOY is my mom upset about it. She's been crying all afternoon. And every time the phone rings she makes Buster say she isn't home. Because she couldn't bear to talk with anyone. She's so ashamed. She'll never live it down. How could I *do* this to her, Superman?

She wept for hours. She sat on the corner of the couch and cried gently, drying her tears with a lace handkerchief. For hours. I wept with her because I couldn't help it. I had never seen her cry like that before—with such sadness. It didn't matter that she was worried about herself more than me. What mattered was that she was worried about herself because of me. Because of ME. I felt so bad. So guilty. I didn't have a chance. Her tears attacked me violently, like Kryptonite, making me helpless, killing me.

You see, I had always cried BECAUSE of her. Never WITH her. Never in the same room with her. There was a communion, so to speak.

Then Veronica came over and my mom couldn't get away and neither could I. So Veronica kept looking at me like I was a piece of dirt or something. And she kept telling my mom how TERRIBLE it was that I could do such a thing. And how she felt so sorry for my mom because EVERYBODY was talking about it. Which my mom already knew. Which Veronica knew my mom already knew. Which is the way Veronica is. She told my mom that she would probably kill herself if one of her kids ever did that. And she kept sticking it in my mom deeper and deeper, again and again, like I was gonna do to my dad. But I'm not anymore. Because if I killed my dad then Veronica would have something more to kill my mom with. And I couldn't stand any more pain, Superman. Especially my mom's pain. I just couldn't.

Your Friend,
JERRY CHARIOT

Dear SUPERMAN,

Robert came by a few minutes ago and asked if I could go out. And my mom said I wasn't allowed. So he said he could come in, but she said he couldn't. So he said he just wanted to help me do our homework. But she said he better GET OUT OF HERE, ROBERT, BEFORE I CALL YOUR MOTHER!

And he said JUST FOR A HALF A HOUR?

And she said NOT EVEN FOR A MINUTE—NOT UNTIL THAT SON OF MINE LEARNS HIS LESSON!

So Robert said BUT HE CAN'T LEARN HIS LESSON UNLESS I HELP HIM but my mom just slammed the door in Robert's face and so he left.

That's why I'm writing this letter, Superman. Because I don't have nothing else to do. Because I'm not allowed to go out and I'm not allowed to watch TV and I'm not allowed to do nothing except my homework which I can't do without Robert anyway. And I'm not gonna get my First Holy Communion until NEXT year which means I'll be seeing a LOT more of Sister Mary Justin who hates me. And I don't get no allowence and I can't buy no comicbooks and I ain't got nothing left, Superman. Except you.

So I hope you'll write back for a change.

Just,

JERRY

DEAR ROBERT,

I decided I would write you a letter since I'm not allowed to talk to you and tell you how I was REAL glad you stopped by today even though it didn't work. Thanks for trying. I even wrote a letter to Superman and told him all about it so he would know. I hope you don't mind. And I was wondering if I could borrow your homework after you're done with it? You could just sneak it in my desk like I'm gonna sneak this letter in yours. And then I'll sneak it back as soon as I'm done with it. Thank you very much. Goodby.

Your friend JERRY

PS: Don't forget to let me know if you got any new comicbooks.

Dear Mr. Editor,

I just wrote a letter to Superman and then I wrote a letter to my bestfriend Robert. But I still have lots of time before I have to go to sleep so I decided I would write another letter and tell you what I think. I think you should let Supergirl have her own comicbook like Superman does. And like Superboy does. And like Superman's Girl Friend Lois Lane and Superman's Pal Jimmy Olsen does. You could call it SUPERMAN'S COUSIN SUPERGIRL. Wouldn't that be good? I think Supergirl's as good as they are and she's a LOT better than Lois Lane that's for sure. And then I'd buy it ALL the time except when I'm broke. And I also hope you'll print this letter in your comicbook so everybody can read it in METROPOLIS MAILBAG. Which is where everybody can write and tell you what they think of your comicbooks. And I think they're very very good.

Thank you very very much.

Sincerly,
Mr. Jerry Chariot

—————

Dear SUPERMAN,

You know what I have to do when everybody else gets to go over to the church and practice their First Holy Communion? I have to go down and sit in the kinder garden where Sister Scholastica gets to watch me all the time. And she's almost as bad as Sister Mary Justin because she makes me sit in the first seat in front of her desk which looks real DUMB because I'm a lot bigger than all those little kinders. Except for one of them named Georgie Gallucci who's real FAT and so nobody likes him anyway. Especially me. Because he saw me writing a letter to Robert Sipanno and he told Sister Scholastica when I was supposed to be doing my Arithmatic. So I really HATE him because she got real mad and made me kneel on my knees in front of the HOLE classroom with a Bible on my head. And she said it better NEVER fall off if I know what's good for me. And then she turned around and started writing on the blackboard and that's when Alfred Sinceri who is Jimmy's little brother threw a paperclip at me. And then Larry Thompson threw a rubberband. And then Georgie Gallucci stuck out his tongue and kept making faces. And then the bell rang Thank God and so I got to go back to Sister Mary Justin's classroom and finish that letter I started to Robert before I got caught. So goodby.

JERRY

DEAR ROBERT,.

Well I did it. I stole that green towel from my mom and I got a Magic Marker and I put KK on it just like I said I was gonna do. And I hid it in the attic right next to where I hide all my old comicbooks. It's too bad you can't get in to see it because it came out REAL nice. That's why I thought I might sneak out on the roof and hold it out so you could stand down on the sidewalk and see it. Except somebody else might see it like Veronica nextdoor who would tell my mom FOR SURE. So maybe you better wait till Sunday. So goodby.

Your Friend,
JERRY

PS: Here's your homework back. I'm sorry I spilt some ink allover it. Jimmy Sinceri made me do it when he kicked my elbow when you was at the blackboard. I tried to wipe it off but it didn't work too good but you can still read quite a bit of it anyway. And you can't read mine too good either.

DEAR SUPERMAN,

The reason Sister Scholastica hates me so much is because Sister Mary Justin hates me so much. Which is also the reason why Sister Agnes Therese the Principle hates me so much. Because if one nunn hates you then they ALL do. And if the nunns don't like you then neither does anybody else. Not even the Protestents or Buster or ANYBODY. That's why he told me I ain't allowed to talk to him EVER again when he sees me on the street sometimes. Because he don't want everybody to think it runs in the family. But I don't care because I hate Buster anyway and the ONLY one I really want to talk to is Robert. Except I can't because my mom won't let me. And neither will Sister Mary Justin. And the only time she ever talks to me anymore is when she wants to say something bad like IT'S TIME TO GO TO THE KINDER GARDEN, JEROME. And today in Religion class she was making all the kids laugh at me like she does all the time now. And she was saying how I was a Pagen just like the Pagens who got drowned in the Red Sea when they was chasing Moses and the Isreelites. Because a Pagen is a person who don't believe in the right God and so the right God (who is God the Father) gets mad and drowns them in the Red Sea.

That's what she said.

So maybe God would make ME get drowned in the Clarion River because the Red Sea's pretty far away from here. But since I know about it now I'll make sure I don't go near the Clarion River for a while. Not until I get Super.

Because then it won't matter if I'm a Pagen or not because if you're Super then you can NEVER get drowned. Not unless there's a piece of Kryptonite at the bottom. Which there won't be because I'll check with my X-ray Vision first. Because God can't kill ME, Superman. Because if you want to be Super then you can't let ANYBODY stop you—not even Sister Mary Justin or your mom or the Holy Ghost or Robert.

Which reminds me.

I had another dream, Superman. I didn't wake up right away and I wasn't alone because Robert was in it. At least I think it was Robert . . .

You see, I walked into this bar that looked a lot like the Italian Club. Except it wasn't, because it was a lot bigger and a lot more crowded. And I saw this man who looked like Robert, except he looked a lot older than Robert. I tried not to stare at him and pretty soon everybody noticed how I was trying not to stare at him. Even he noticed.

So I went into the men's room and I peed and I looked into the mirror for a long time and I washed my hands and I dried them and when I went back he was still there. Sipping a beer.

So I ordered a Bud and I stood in a corner and I watched him drinking his drink and I wondered when I was gonna wake up. I mean, what's a kid like me doing in a place like this? Look at all these people. Look at all these men. They're ALL looking for Robert. Their own Robert. What am I doing here? I should be home writing a letter or something.

But I can't leave now.

I can't take my eyes off that guy that looks like Robert. Do you see him over there? He's the one with the red shirt and the perfect blue eyes. I'd know them anywhere. See how they won't look back? See how they look through me? It's as if he's never seen me before. He doesn't know that it's me. Jerry. The kid who became The Kid. Hey,

Robert, LOOK! Please, Robert! (He's ignoring me. He can't hear the look on my face.) Hey, Robert! Look at me! Before I wake up! HURRY!

. . . It was AWFUL, Superman. One of the WORST dreams I ever had. That's why I was afraid to go back to sleep. So I took out a sheet of paper and I started writing this letter. And pretty soon I'm gonna write a letter to the editor of your comicbooks. And then maybe I'll write another letter to Robert Sipanno. And then it'll be time to wake up and go to school and kneel in front of Sister Scholastica's classroom again. So goodby for now. And goodnight.

Your friend,
JERRY CHARIOT

***

Dear Mr. Editor,

I been reading your comicbooks ever since I learned how to read. And before that I used to look at the pictures quite a bit. So I know a awful lot about Superman and Jimmy Olsen and Everybody Else. Even Lois Lane and Mr. Mxyzptlk! who lives in The Fifth Dimension. And I even wrote a letter to METROPOLIS MAILBAG which I'm still waiting to hear about. So I thought it would be a good idea if you hired me to write stories about Superman when I get to Metropolis. I mean print because I don't write very good yet. But even Sister Mary Justin in school said I'm a REAL good printer and so if you hired me then I could go out and talk to Superman and ask him what he's been doing lately. And then I'll come back to the office and write (I mean print) about it. And somebody else can draw the pictures because I don't draw too good. And then you could put it in your comicbooks because you always print anyway. And you print REAL NICE just like I do. Except I print a little bigger. So the pictures are gonna have to be smaller. So I hope that's OK. Goodnight.

Sincerly Yours Truly,
MR. JERRY CHARIOT

PS: I almost forgot to tell you that my friend Robert Sipanno is gonna be coming to Metropolis with me and you might want to meet him because he prints pretty good also. And so maybe he could print about SUPERMAN'S PAL JIMMY OLSEN if you want.

Dear Robert,

On Sunday morning I'll say I forgot something when we're getting in the car to go watch everybody else get their First Holy Communion. Because my mom said I have to go anyway because that's part of my punishment. And so I'll run upstairs and I'll go right in the attic and I'll get my cape and put it on and climb out on the roof. And my dad'll be in the car saying WHERE IN THE HELL IS THAT BOY? And he'll probly be thinking about hitting me. And so I'll go right to the edge where EVERYBODY can see me and I'll look down and yell HERE I AM! Except Buster will be in the back seat so I'll have to wait until he climbs out.

And looks up.

And sees me standing on the roof with my arms out in front of me and my cape flapping behind me.

And maybe Veronica nextdoor will be coming out of her house and so she'll get to see me also. And then if you

148

and your family was coming down the street at the same time then you'd get to see it too, Robert. EVERYBODY could see me jump, leap, soar through the air like on TV. And I'll fly right down towards my mom and she'll say LOOK!

And my dad'll say UP IN THE SKY!

And Buster'll say IT'S A BIRD!

And Veronica will yell IT'S A PLANE!

And then it would be your turn, Robert. And so you could say NO, IT'S THE KRYPTONITE KID!

Isn't that good?

Your BESTfriend,
JERRY

I had another dream last night. It was the worst one yet. I dreamed I wasn't big anymore. I dreamed I was little and I was still a kid and I was standing on the roof and I was alone. Nobody was there except me and my cape and I didn't know who I was. And I didn't know when I was. And I was crying because I couldn't find Robert. "ROBERT!" I cried. "ROBERT, WHERE ARE YOU?" Nobody answered. Not at first. Then I heard a voice, a small voice coming from below. I looked down.

I saw Robert.

He was lying on the ground, clutching a crucifix, looking up at me with fear, with a helmet—looking up at me as if I were the last thing he would ever see. And crying.

And each tear was a different color.

And then I jumped. I leaped straight toward him. I fell through the air like a grenade.

I woke up.

DEAR ROBERT,

What I thought I'd do is fly down and pick you up and give you a ride to Holy Redeemer Church. Right in front of your mom and my mom and EVERYBODY. Then I'll go fly around for a while and I'll wait until all the people get inside. Especially Sister Mary Justin. Then I'll fly in and land right on the altar, right below the statue of The Virgin Mary, and I'll let the HOLE church look at me for a while. And I won't even care when they start whispering and talking and pointing as I fly up in the air like the Holy Ghost and pee on Sister Mary Justin. And then I'll pee on Jimmy Sinceri and Janie Jobb and Duane Machado and Sister Scholastica and Pastor Ponti. Then I'll fly around again, flying closer, right over Sister Mary Justin's veil, like a helicopter, and I'll poop on her.

Right on her head!

Because it won't matter anymore, Robert. Nothing will matter anymore because we won't need anybody. Not even our moms or our dads or The Baby Jesus or ANYBODY! Because we'll have each other, Robert. We'll love each other. We'll fly everywhere and do everything. Like Batman and Robin. Like Peter Pan and Tinkerbell. Like Superman and Jimmy Olsen. We'll be a team. Pals!

At last, Robert—just you and me! JERRY and ROBERT! Nobody else!

Except Superman.

Love,Love,LOVE,
JERRY

The
Fifth
Dimension

Dear Superman,

How are you? My name is Robert Sipanno and I am fine thank you. But Jerry isn't. He's right here beside me. We're both writing you this letter. Only I'm doing the writing because he can't. He isn't allowed to move his arms because the doctor won't let him. And neither will the nurse. She keeps coming around and checking on him and giving him pills and that's why I'm writing it. Only Jerry keeps telling me everything I'm supposed to write down and I write it write away. So this letter is really from me and not Robert. Isn't that right, Robert? Maybe we better start all over again.

DEAR SUPERMAN,

My name is Robert Sipanno and I'm the one who's writing I mean printing this letter. But I'm not the one who's REALLY writing it because this is the way we do it. Jerry says something and then I write it down. And then he says something else and I write it down. That's the way we do it. So that means that Jerry is really doing the writing and I'm just doing the printing. Only I don't print too good so I hope you can read it OK. Because I'm sitting in a chair and Jerry is laying down in bed. He can't sit up. He can't even have a pillow. In fact he has to lay there looking at the ceiling and he can't even get up to pee.

Maybe we shouldn't tell him that, Robert. In fact he has to lay there looking at the ceiling and he can't even get up

153

to go look out the window. That's better. Superman will figure it out.

And that's why Jerry can't do the printing because he hurt his arms. And also his legs and everything else. Except his face. That's the only thing that's not all wrapped up. So he has to stay here with the nurses and the nunns all the time. And they wouldn't let me in at first because they said I was too little. But then they changed their minds. That's why Jerry hasn't written you a letter in a LONG time, Superman. Because I wasn't here to do it for him. But now I am. And this is it.

So we hope you like it.

Goodby.

Your friends, Jerry and Robert.

How did that sound, Robert? Did you get it all down? I hope I didn't talk too fast. Maybe you better hold it up so I can see it. Robert? Are you still there, Robert? Hey, ROBERT! Will you please stop writing and

———※———

Dear SUPERMAN,

Why don't you change that to Man of Steel?

Dear MAN OF STEEL,

I've been here quite a while now. In fact it's almost a month. Or maybe even more. At first the only person who was allowed to come in was grown ups like my mom and dad. Except my dad never comes but I don't care anyway. All I cared about was Robert but they said he couldn't. And I said Why? And they said Because he's too little and little kids aren't allowed in here unless they get sick or jump off a building. Which I wouldn't advise.

So one day one of the nunns came over to my bed and said her name was Sister Madonna. That's what she said. And I didn't say anything back to her right away because she was a nunn and you know about them. But it turned out she was a real nice nunn which is probably why she got to wear a white outfit. Sister Mary Justin always wears a black one. So Sister Madonna told me how there was this cute little kid outside and he wanted to come in but he couldn't So would you please give this present to my friend Jerry please? Then she smiled just like The Virgin Mary when she looks at The Baby Jesus in our Catechism. Then she gave it to me. Only I couldn't open it because my hands are all wrapped up like the present. So Sister Madonna said she would do it and she did it. And you'll NEVER guess what it was, Superman? It was SUPERMAN'S PAL JIMMY OLSEN NO. 77! I couldn't believe it!

"Gosh!" I said, and I almost jumped up. But I couldn't. There's this big thing all over my chest.

"Oh, be careful!" she said urgently, as if the pain that suddenly shot through me was hers, not mine.

I looked up at her.

"Will you read it to me?" I asked. "Please? Oh, please? You GOT to. I can't read it myself. Oh PLEASE?"

She smiled, then folded her hands like she was going to pray. Then she said, "Surely."

Robert would have just said, "Sure."

First she read me a whole page and then she held up the comicbook so I could see all the pictures. And then she read me another page and that's the way we did it. I thought it was pretty good, especially the story about TITANO who was a giant gorilla who had Kryptonite eyes. And so if he looked at Superman then he might kill you. And that's why you couldn't stop him and so Jimmy Olsen had to do it. Because Titano kept stepping on people and climbing up the side of The Daily Planet so Jimmy decided to drink some of that Magic Stuff that made him grow REAL big. Real quick. And on page six he was even bigger than Titano or The Daily Planet or ANYTHING. And that's how he got rid of that awful ape. And then it said THE AND. I mean END. And then Sister Madonna said, "Did you like it?"

And I said, "Sure, didn't you?"

And she said, "Well if you did, then I did."

And I said, "What if I didn't?"

And she said, "Then I would feel bad because I want you to be happy." And she smiled her smile.

And I said, "Who do you think you're kidding?"

And she said, "Myself."

Then she made the Sign of the Cross and left.

And I thought: Gee, I wished I would've had some of that Magic Stuff when I jumped. Then I could've been real BIG and I wouldn't have fallen so far. Then I would've showed them!

But I didn't, Superman. I fell, Superman.

———⋈———

I fell asleep and I was standing on top of my dad's apartment building and everybody was watching me and I had my green cape on and I felt so good. And I felt so beautiful. And I was looking down at everybody. And I was just bending down, just getting ready to leap in the air, when allofasudden my mom yelled, "LOOK!"

And my dad yelled, "UP IN THE SKY!"

And Buster yelled, "IT'S A BIRD!"

And Veronica yelled, "IT'S A PLANE!"

And Robert yelled, "NO—IT'S SUPERMAN!"

And sure enough, it was.

You came zooming out of the sky like a star, shooting straight toward me. I could hardly believe it! It was REALLY you, Superman! I HAD to wave at you! I couldn't help it. I had to yell, "HI, SUPERMAN! I'M OVER HERE! COME AND GET ME, SUPERMAN!" And you did. You flew down and picked me up and held me in your arms and we started flying away. And I waved goodbye to EVERYBODY—to my mom, and my dad, and Veronica. And I spit on Buster and it landed right in his hair. And I waved goodbye to Robert. And I yelled, "DON'T WORRY, ROBERT! WE'LL BE BACK TO GET YOU!" And then allofasudden my eyes turned into Kryptonite just like that giant ape's and they started hurting you, Superman. And you started falling to the ground. And I started falling with you. And Buster started laughing. And we kept falling, falling together, crashing to the earth. Together! And I tried to look away so I wouldn't hurt you, Superman. So I wouldn't kill you. But I COULDN'T take my Kryptonite eyes off you! You were so beautiful. So perfect. And you were MINE—at last! I couldn't look away!

———❦———

I woke up screaming. Sister Madonna was standing beside my bed, praying. Her hands were folded. Her head was tilted to one side. She reached out and touched me gently, on the forehead, with her smile. She said, "Poor child, what is it? What's troubling you?" She dried my tears with her handkerchief because I couldn't do it myself, I couldn't

157

move my arms, or my feet. I couldn't turn my head. I could only look up, at the ceiling, which was dark. "Can I get you anything?" she asked. "Do you want anything?" I tried to move my lips, to explain, to tell her there's only one thing:

"I want to fly."

I didn't say it. Instead I said:

"Can you do me a favor?"
And she said, "What is it, my child?"
And I told her how I was glad she was praying for me and everything but couldn't she maybe check and see if Robert could get in to see me? And she said Who's Robert? And I said He's the one who's writing this letter because I'm just doing the talking. He's the one who brought me that comicbook. And she said she would talk to the doctor and see what she could do God willing.

"Now get some rest," she said, kissing my eyes.

But how could I sleep, Superman? There were so many things going on inside me. There were so many things I HAD to tell you because a lot of things have changed, Superman. You see, I've learned something— I've learned something VERY important. I've been laying here for weeks now, just looking at the ceiling and counting the cracks and waiting for something to happen. Like maybe they'll let Robert in. I sure hope so. I can't STAND it anymore, Superman. They got me tied up like a mummy. I can't turn my neck. I can't turn anything. I feel like I'm frozen.

Sister Madonna whispered to somebody that I broke my neck poor child. But I don't believe it. I don't believe ANYTHING anymore, Superman. Not even you.

Every time my mom comes in she has to stick her neck way over so I can see her face. The bandages go all around my face and it's like looking out of a window all the time. Except the window's in the roof because I have to look up all the time. And every time my mom cries my face gets all wet and sometimes tears fall from her eyes into my eyes.

And she cries a lot, Superman. Almost every time she comes.

Which is everyday.

She always brings me a present. And usually it's a pretty nice one like a sailboat. Which I can't play with anyway because I'm not allowed to take a bath. Because I can't. And she always wears a black dress which she NEVER did before. She sits beside me on the bed, gently, as if I might crack. She bends over me and smiles and asks me how I am and I never answer. I never say a word to her, not since I've been here. She keeps talking the whole time, telling me about Buster and the new hot water heater and everything. And usually I listen but I never talk. Not to her. Not to her or Buster or my sister the Sister or anybody. They even let my sister get away from the convent so she could come and try to talk to me. Which she did. "Why won't you talk to us?" she asked. "Why won't you talk to mom? It's killing her." But I didn't say anything, Superman. I just looked up at the ceiling and I didn't even smile. When she was leaving she said she would pray for me.

I decided something, Superman. I decided there's a LOT of people I don't want to talk to anymore. So I'm not. I'm just going to lay here and look at the ceiling and wait. I'll wait here in darkness for the morning. I'll wait here in mourning for the evening. I'll watch the electric lights go on, then off. Then the nurse will say, "It's time for your midnight pill. Wake up." And I'll say to myself:

I am awake.

The doctor is standing at the foot of my bed. I can't see him, but I can feel him. I can hear him talking. His voice sounds distant, like a bad phone connection. I can't hear too well with these bandages over my ears. Sister Madonna is to my left. She's talking louder, as if she's interpreting what the doctor says. She's looking down on me. I can see the top of her head. I think it's morning and I think I'm awake. Sometimes I'm not too sure. The ceiling is bright. A ray of sunlight is shooting through the window beside me, like a searchlight. I can feel the warmth on my shoulder.

Sister Madonna is talking but the doctor is speaking.

He says he is moving me to another room where it will be OK if Robert comes in to see me. And he says he is going to send in another doctor who wants to look at me. Only he doesn't want to give me shots or anything. He just wants to talk to me sometimes. And I never heard of a doctor who didn't give any shots but I said OK because I didn't have much choice. I REALLY wanted to see Robert so he could write this letter. And also just because I wanted to see him. So that meant I had to see the other doctor who didn't know how to give shots. Whose name was Dr. Clark.

"Nice name," I said.

He looked puzzled.

"I just like the name Clark," I said.

"Well, gee, thanks Jerry."

"You're welcome."

He tried to be real friendly and talked as if he was a kid just like I was. Which was pretty dumb, I thought. He smiled a lot but it never stayed there very long because he kept asking another question. I didn't like him too much.

He asked me why I wouldn't talk to my mom?

"I don't want to."

He said What's wrong, don't you like your mom?

"She's OK."

He said Well what about your dad?

"I hate him."

He said Do you ever dream about him?

"No, but . . ."

"But what?"

"But I dreamed about my mom the other day."

"What was it?"

"It's pretty hard to explain."

"Try."

"OK."

And then I told him how

I was laying on the ground and my green cape was twisted all around my neck and my mom was crying. She was crying and screaming "WHY? WHY DID HE DO IT?"

Veronica tried to hold her back, but she kept coming closer and closer. She kept looking at me and screaming to everybody, "Why? Oh God, *WHY*?" She held on to that question like a crucifix. And then I heard the siren.

And then I woke up, Dr. Clark.

———————✖———————

There was sweat all over my forehead. I could feel it dripping in my eyes. Sister Madonna wasn't around like she usually is. It was the middle of the night. I tried to call the nurse but I could hardly talk. My throat was real dry. There was nothing I could do. I lay there trapped inside my bandages. Pretty soon I fell asleep again. What else could I do? It was too dark to see the cracks. There was no one there to talk to. I closed my eyes and heard the siren.

It kept getting louder and louder. And closer. There was a whole bunch of people around me, looking at me and making funny faces. My eyes were open and I could watch them. But I couldn't hear them. All I could hear was the siren. It was right next to me. Then it stopped. They were picking me up and putting me in. Buster was standing right there watching. He wasn't saying nothing. He looked like he was gonna throw up. He was even crying a little bit. But not as much as my mom. But quite a bit for Buster. Somebody said, "Be careful! Don't hurt him!" I tried to tell them that it didn't hurt, that I was numb, I couldn't feel anything. But words wouldn't come out. It felt like some-body was sitting on my throat. I could hardly open my mouth. So I didn't. I watched them close the doors. They slammed them shut. The last word I heard belonged to my mom. "*Why?*" It got caught in the door. And then the siren.

And then I woke up.

———⸭———

Robert was sitting next to the bed, waiting for me. Sister Madonna was touching my cheek.

"Your friend is here," she said softly into my ear. "Come on, my child. He's waiting."

She smiled her saintly smile, then helped Robert onto the bed beside me. That's so he could look down at my face and I could see him. He isn't too big either, you know. He's the second shortest boy in the class. Aren't you, Robert? So he looked down at my eyes and I looked up at his eyes and then he said, "Hi."

So I said, "Hi."

(And that's all we said for a long time. We just looked at each other. He was wearing a uniform and he was carrying a gun. That's what he told me. Said he might not be back. I laughed. "Sure you will," I said. He smiled. Then he said he loved me. Then he got mortared. Then I woke up.)

———⸭———

"I really liked the comicbook," I told him.

"So did I."

"I thought the story about the gorilla was real good."

"Yeah."

Then he said:

"You can keep it if you want."

Then I said:

"Thanks, Robert."

Then we didn't say anything for a while.

You see, Superman, it was really hard to talk to him. Because I hadn't seen him for a LONG time and so I didn't know what to say. So many things have changed since I last saw him. You know, the fall and everything. It was almost as if we were strangers, meeting for the first time beneath a cracked ceiling. Except we weren't really strangers because we knew we were gonna be friends because we used to be. And because we need to be. Isn't that right, Robert?

Then after a while Sister Madonna said she had to go pray but I think she had to go pee. Anyway she left. And me and Robert started talking a lot faster and he told me how EVERYBODY's been talking about it. And Duane Machado said the reason I jumped was because I was trying to commit suicide just like you did way back when we was eating pork chops. Remember? And Jimmy Sinceri said he was GLAD I jumped. And Janie Jobb said that she was too but she'd never say it BECAUSE YOU'RE NOT SUPPOSED TO. And Robert said he heard Sister Mary Justin whisper how there was a Devil in my body. And it pushed me off and tried to kill me so it could take me to HELL.

But they're all WRONG, Superman. Nobody knows why I REALLY did it. Not even Robert, who said he heard his mom talking to Veronica on the telephone about how my mom was losing weight. And about how she was going through Hell and they hope she don't lose the baby. What they was talking about was my baby brother who will turn out to be my baby sister. If she makes it.

And Robert said my mom NEVER goes out of the house except when she has to go to the hospital or church. And she always goes to the early Mass because it's at 6 o'clock in the morning and so there's hardly anybody there. Because one time I went when my brother Buster was starting to be a altarboy. And so he had to work the early shift because he was a new altarboy and all the older altarboys didn't like getting up so early. And neither did I. But my mom said I had to. And Buster was pretty good except one time he sneezed when he was supposed to say Amen. And so I laughed and my mom hit me. And another time he was going up the altarsteps when he dropped some incense on the priest's foot. So he bent down to pick it up and the priest started to genuflect and he knocked Buster down the steps. It wouldn't have been too bad except he landed on the other altarboy who was holding a candle. And the wax fell on Buster's neck and he yelled REAL loud and jumped up and knocked over the statue of Saint Dominic. And the head of Saint Dominic broke off and rolled down the aisle and landed near the fourth pew. And the nose broke off also. It landed near the seventh pew where Mary Louise was sitting. She looked down at it. I heard a siren.

I woke up.

Robert was still beside me on the bed. The room was dark. The nurse was gone. I heard something rattling down the hallway. Robert held me closer. Then he started whispering in my ear.

"You said something when you jumped," he said. "I heard you say something. You were laying on the ground and you were mumbling and everybody was standing around but nobody could understand. Nobody knew what you were saying, what you were trying to do. Except for me, Jerry. I'm your bestfriend. I knew. But I didn't tell anybody. I stood there looking at your face. It was twisted way back and there was blood in your hair. But your eyes were open and you were awake. You weren't dreaming. You kept looking at your mom who was crying. You kept saying that one word over and over—that one word nobody could understand. Not even Veronica nextdoor. HE'S DELERIOUS, she said. HE'S NOT SAYING ANYTHING. But she was wrong, as usual. I knew what you were saying, Jerry. I understood what you were trying to do when you looked up so helplessly and said

!kltpzyxM

"And then you heard a siren."

"Is that all you can remember?" Dr. Clark asked.

"Yes," I said. "Yes, that's all."

"Do you know what it means, Jerry? This word—what is it?—Kilipzim or Kilpitzim or . . ."

"*!kltpzyxM*" I said. "It's *!kltpzyxM*—accent on the second syllable."

"Yes, *!kltpzyxM* . . . Would you mind spelling that for me?"

"Sure, it's ! k l t p z y . . ."

And then I stopped.

And then I looked at Dr. Clark.

And then I said: "Hey, you're not trying to trick me, are you?"

"Trick you?"

"YES! You're trying to make me spell my name backwords! You're trying to send me to The Fifth Dimension!"

"What are you talking about?" the doctor asked, and a look of panic spread across his face. He pressed the buzzer beside my bed.

"YOU KNOW WHAT I'M TALKING ABOUT!" I said much louder, almost shouting. "You're trying to trick me! You're not really a doctor! You're pretending! That's why you don't give shots! This whole thing's just an act. You're trying to get rid of me. You're not a doctor! You're SUPER-MAN!"

He froze.

He put down his pen.

He looked me right in the eyes, then took off his glasses.

"You've figured me out this time," he said, unbuttoning his shirt.

I gave him one of my impish smiles.

"Don't worry, Mr. Mxyzptlk! I'll get you yet!" he said, unzipping his fly and pulling off his pants. He stood there beside my bed in full uniform. He reached across my fragile body and opened the window. "I'll get you yet!" he shouted, then leaped out the window, into the air, sucking the curtains behind him. He left me there alone, with my bandages.

"I'LL GET YOU YET, MR. MXYZPTLK!" he shouted behind him.

Suddenly there were three nurses around my bed. Dr. Clark was shouting orders to them, but I couldn't hear. There was this noise in my ears, like a siren. I couldn't breathe too good. I saw a needle flash before my eyes, then I felt it going into my neck. Deep into my neck. The last thing I heard was my mom's voice. "WHY?" it asked.

And then the doors slammed.

And then I woke up.

Robert was still beside me, writing this letter. But then Sister Madonna came in and told him it's time to go young man. And that's why we have to stop write here, Superman. Because Sister Madonna's waiting. Time's up. But Robert will be back tomorrow and we'll write you another letter then. So don't worry.

Goodbye.

Your friends,
JERRY and ROBERT

OK, Robert, are you ready? DEAR SUPERMAN,

How are you? I am fine thank you. Considering the circumstances. Robert is pretty good too. He just got here a few minutes ago and we decided to write you a letter RIGHT away. This way we might finish it before Sister Madonna comes back. Which is why I told Robert he better write faster this time—huh, Robert? Isn't that right, Robert? Robert, are you there?

Robert?

Yoo-hooooo, Robert!

(*Or are you in some other dimension?*)

What can I do, Superman? He keeps writing down EVERYTHING I say. HEY, *ROBERT!* RoooooooBERT! See? Nothing works. Damn!

HEY, you with the freckles all over your cheeks! You with the pen in your hand! Hey, Robert—I know something you don't know.

I know when you're gonna DIE, Robert! I DO! I saw it in a dream and I'm gonna tell you if you don't stop write now! Do you hear?

Christ, Superman, if I could only get out of these bandages. If I could only reach out and take that pen away. But I can't move. I'm trapped!

OK, Robert, this is your last chance. If you don't stop pretty soon it's ALL gonna be over. EVERYTHING!

Don't you see, Robert? You're gonna die as soon as they catch us.

As soon as they arm you with guilt.

So you better stop NOW. Please, Robert . . . Please stop . . . ROBERT! I don't want you to die.

(*I don't want you to get mortared.*)

Please, Robert . . . Oh, God. Robert. Oh Jesus, Robert, that feels good. Ohhhhhhhhhhh, my God, Robert! Faster! FASTER! Oh, Robert! Oh..... Oh. Robert! Oh..... *OhhhhhhhhhhhhhhhhhhhHHHHHHHHHHHHHHHHHHHHHHHHHH HHHHHHHHHHHHHHHHHHHHHHHHHHHHHHHHHHH!*

———⟡———

DEAR SUPERMAN,

Now where were we? Oh, yes! I wanted to tell you about how I felt like a gorilla trapped on top of a big building. Like King Kong.

Except I was a person and not a gorilla like Titano.

169

And I was wearing a cape. Gorillas don't usually wear capes. But I was. But still I felt like a gorilla—like Mighty Joe Young, if that's possible. Which it is because EVERYBODY down below was running around and screaming and pointing up at me.

And my mom was yelling GODDAMNIT, JERRY, GET DOWN HERE!

And my dad ran inside the house and so I KNEW he was coming up on the roof and I had to do it quick. I heard Buster say, AWW, HE'S CHICKEN ANYWAY! and Veronica said real loud like she always does, MYGOD! THAT BOY'S CRAZY! There was more commotion than you could imagine, Superman! EVERYBODY was doing something—yelling something!

I heard my dad's feet pounding up the steps, getting nearer.

They stomped, they yelled, they screamed at me. They kept coming at me from every direction—like airplanes!—trying to knock me off! The WHOLE neighborhood was there. Everybody was watching. And laughing. And pointing. EVERYBODY!

And right in the middle of them all was ROBERT! Only he wasn't yelling or anything. He was just looking up at me, and smiling. I saw his teeth sparkle in the sunlight. I saw his blue eyes shining like halos. He looked so innocent, so calm—like a tree on a battlefield. I smiled back. I looked down. I couldn't take my eyes off him.

I heard my dad's footsteps climbing up on the roof, rushing toward me. Quickly! Urgently!

My mom yelled BE CAREFUL!

Everybody down below was allofasudden quiet. Watching. Waiting. I looked down at them ALL! I looked at Robert again. I saw his smile. I smiled BIGGER. I felt my dad's fingertips reaching out. I heard my mom yell OH MY GOD! *MY GOD!* And then it happened.

<hr>

I woke up. Dr. Clark was sitting on the chair beside my bed.

"But there must be more!" he said.

"No," I said. "I always wake up. I never hit the ground. It's always the same, Dr. Clark."

"Are you sure?"

"Sure I'm sure."

"But wasn't there something else?" he said. "Didn't you say something about a midget or something? I'm sure you did."

"I don't know what you're talking about."

"Surely you remember," he said. "Something about—ah, here it is! The name is Mr. Mxyzptlk! I believe. Am I pronouncing that correctly?"

"It's close enough."

"Well, according to you," he said, turning a page, "this Mxyzptlk! character is a white male, about 33 years old, with . . ."

"That's inches."

"What?"

"He's 33 inches high. I don't know how old he is."

"I see. Thank you. . . . About 33 inches high, with red hair and a funny purple hat. Comes from a place called The Fifth Dimension, which we can't seem to locate at the moment. Both of his parents are confirmed imps. And not only are they confirmed, but they also received their First Holy Communion. No one seems to know his first name, and no one seems to be able to pronounce his last. He's a slippery character. Sometimes goes by the name of *!kltpzyxM* when he wants to make a quick getaway. Seems to have a fetish about making Superman unhappy or something?"

"Miserable," I said. "He wants to make Superman miserable."

"Yes, miserable. How do you spell that?"

"Ms. erable," I said.

"Yes, that's it. Thank you. Well now, according to what you said, this Mxyzptlk character . . ."

"You forgot the exclamation point."

"Oh. Sorry . . . This Mxyzptlk! character has a thing about spelling his name backwords. Says it can make him disappear, is that right?"

"That's it."

"But why does he want to disappear?"

"Oh, he doesn't WANT to—he HAS to. Whenever he gets tricked."

"I'm afraid I don't understand."

"It's really easy," I said. "You see, Mr. Mxyzptlk! lives in this place called The Fifth Dimension and . . ."

"Yes, The Fifth Dimension. I like that. It's got a nice ring to it. The Fifth Dimension. Where is it, can you tell me?"

"Sure. It's where nobody has any cars and everybody's a imp, and so if you want to go somewhere all you have to do is say your name backwords. And if you don't want to go anywhere you don't. That's why you have to trick him."

"Hmmmm," he said. "I think you misunderstood my question."

"I usually do."

"What I meant was: Where is The Fifth Dimension? Is it outside Cincinnati, Ohio? Or is it near the Duck Rock? Or is it in Vietnam?"

"Oh!" I said. "You mean, where is it located?"

"Yes! That's it! Where is it exactly?"

"It's exactly between The Fourth Dimension and The Sixth Dimension."

"Hmmmmmm," he said again, looking at me for a long time. And then he said:

"What's a dimension, Jerry?"

"A dimension is what you live in."

"How many dimensions are there?"

"Thousands."

"Name some."

"Sure. Let's start with The Zero Dimension. That's God. And The First Dimension is angels and The Second Dimension is comicbooks. The Third Dimension is Hell, I'm certain of it. The Fourth Dimension is poetry and The Fifth Dimension is imps. I don't know what's in The Sixth Dimension, but The Seventh Dimension is pork chops and The Eighth Dimension is . . ."

"Thank you, Jerry."

"You're welcome, Dr. Clark."

"Can I ask you something, Jerry?"

"Sure. Anything."

"Why did you pick The Fifth Dimension when you jumped?"

"You mean when I found out I couldn't fly."

"Yes. Why did you try to disappear to The Fifth Dimension? Why not, say, The Sixth Dimension, or The Seventh Dimension?"

"I already told you."

"You did?"

"Yes, I didn't know what was in The Sixth Dimension and I'd rather be with the imps than the pork chops."

"I see," he said, taking off his glasses and rubbing his eyes. And then I said:

"I don't think you can see ANYTHING, Dr. Clark! You keep looking at ME—at my face, at my bandages. You keep asking what does THIS mean? What does THAT mean?

"I want you to have X-ray Vision, Dr. Clark!

"I want you to look INSIDE me. Can you see it? It's the answer to EVERYTHING I am! It's my mom and my dad and Buster and Veronica and Sister Mary Justin and Robert and his smile, his perfect smile, looking up at me, at my cape, at my dad, on the roof, reaching out . . .

"BLAME THEM! They're ALL inside me, Dr. Clark, trapped like words on a page . . . "

(Look around some more, Dr. Clark. Crawl inside my bones. Flow inside my veins. Can you see it? It's the answer to EVERY-THING I am! It's Lois Lane and Jimmy Olsen and Perry White and Krypto and Mr. Mxyzptlk! And Superman, of course. They're ALL there, Dr. Clark! They're all REAL, too! They keep appearing out of nowhere, like keys from a typewriter, one after another . . .)

Are you still there, Dr. Clark? Can you see them? Can you see how they're looking up at me, pointing at me? Can you see my dad reaching out, trying to stop me?

Can you see my green cape? Isn't it pretty?

Are you watching, Dr. Clark? Go ahead, make your way through the crowd. Don't step on Mr. Mxyzptlk! That's it, put your glasses on. Nobody will bother you. They're all watching me and my dad on the roof. Now stop a minute. Stand there beside my mom. See the look of panic on her face? Can you hear the word she's hurling out of her mouth with such horror?

Look at her, Dr. Clark. Help HER, not me! She needs it.

They ALL need it, Dr. Clark. It's too late for me.

I've already jumped. I'm already falling to the ground helplessly. Can you hear the look on my face? Can you see the words in my mouth? I'm saying *!kltpzyxM*. I'm saying *!toirahC*. I'm looking for the word—the one word that might save me!

Where is it, Dr. Clark?

I'm even saying my first name—*!yrreJ*—but it doesn't work! I tried EVERYTHING. I tried rearranging the letters in my name. *!itchorA*, I said. *!hotricA*, I yelled. But nothing happened. I didn't disappear. What can I do? The ground keeps rushing toward me, violently toward me, like a door in my face. What's wrong?

Help me, Dr. Clark! Help me!

Listen to me: *!cathirO*, I'm yelling. *!architO*, I'm yelling. I'm still falling . . .

Help me, Robert! Save me, Superman! Oh God, what's the word? Is it *!chortiA?* Is it *!aihcroT?* Is it . . .

Hey. Hey, that's it!

I found it! I'm doing it! I'm disa p
p
e
a
r
i

n

"You certainly are, Jerry."

"Sorry, doctor. Sometimes I get excited and fly off the handle."

"The handle? I thought you flew off the roof?"

"No, I didn't fly off the roof."

"Then you jumped?"

"No, I didn't jump either."

"Then what happened?"

"Nothing. I was chicken."

"You mean . . ."

"I mean I lied. I didn't jump. I didn't fly. I waited too long. My dad reached out. He grabbed me. He held me in his arms real tight, almost hurting me. He was crying. My dad was crying! And then he did something that he never did before."

"And what was that?"

"He kissed me."

"And then what happened?"

"I grew up."

"And then what happened?"

"I woke up."

Robert was gone. The room was dark, except for a dim light from the hallway. Sister Madonna was standing beside my bed, praying. I couldn't see her, but I knew she was there. A nurse came in with my midnight pill. I closed my eyes and pretended I was asleep.

"How is he?" the nurse whispered.

"Better," the nun whispered.

"Poor kid," the nurse whispered. "Did you tell him yet?"

"No," the nun whispered. "I haven't found the right words."

"Maybe you should wait till tomorrow?" the nurse whispered.

"Yes, maybe I will," the nun whispered.

"Poor kid," the nurse whispered again. And then she reached out to awaken me.

When the nurse was gone, Sister Madonna stood there for a long time in silence. In darkness. I knew she was crying because I could hear her tears hitting the floor. They sounded distant, like a dream remembered (for an instant) in the afternoon. Her tears came from God, like everything else.

"I know what it is," I said. *I know what you want to tell me.* She was silent.

"I had this dream," I said. "I was falling through the air. Somebody was holding me in his arms. I had a green cape on and we kept falling, falling together, crashing to the earth. Together. At first I thought it was Superman— that he had swooped down and tried to save me. But it wasn't. It was my dad. He realized he couldn't reach me, so he leaped. Like Superman. He caught me in mid-air and fell with me, in front of me, saving me from the sidewalk. But not from the siren."

I woke up.

Sister Madonna was still standing there, crying. Looking at me. Praying. Saying over and over, "God forgive him. God forgive this child, this child." She was like a guardian angel in the night. She waited until she was sure I was asleep, then tip-toed away silently. I heard her pause at the door. I wanted to tell her that it didn't hurt, that I was numb, I couldn't feel anything. But words wouldn't come out. I felt like somebody was sitting on my throat. I could hardly open my mouth. So I didn't. I heard her close the door. She squeezed it shut, gently. The last word I heard belonged to my mom. *"WHY?"* It got caught in the door.

And then the siren.

I've been having tons of crisp dreams lately, waking with the sunlight and remembering every horrid detail. They're full of heavy chunks of past, of old faces floating through the air, exploding into punctuation marks. Every night they occur, like mosquitoes biting into my sleep, leaving marks that will itch all morning, all afternoon, all the way into evening, by which time I feel a compulsion to record them. But when I sit down at my desk and confront an empty sheet of paper, they run away like children. I chase them and they laugh. I sip my coffee. I nervously light a cigarette. I say a prayer. I bless myself. I slide between my sheets and crawl inside my sleep with certainty. I know they will come again. I know they will find me . . .

The And

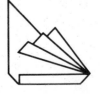